The Last Frame

FRAMES OF FEAR

CEDAR JAMES

NORTH & ANCHOR, CO.

Published by North & Anchor Co., Houston, TX

Cover by Q Designs

Artwork and Graphic Design by Syn Li

ISBN: 979-8-9987306-5-8

ASIN: B0GX2WXQC2

✿ Formatted with Vellum

For my readers,
Thank you for following me into darker waters.
And for embracing the roots of my writing.
Thriller and suspense are the very foundation from which my career
was born. I hope you find beauty in the tension, the longing, the
ruin, the truth hiding in the shadows, the ache, and the raw, restless
heart of my darker side.

Your trust and faith in me mean more than I can ever properly say.
I hope this story gets under your skin in all the best ways.

Content Warning

Thank you for picking up *The Last Frame*. This story lives in the dark. It is a romantic thriller rooted in obsession, voyeurism, violation, desire, fear, and the dangerous intimacy of being truly seen by the wrong person. Because I want you to step into this book with your eyes open, I'm gently offering a content note before you begin.

Please be aware that this book contains:
- serial murder
- stalking and obsessive surveillance
- voyeurism
- home invasion
- nonconsensual photography, including a sleeping woman being photographed without her knowledge
- repeated invasion of privacy and violation of personal safety
- strangulation/manual strangulation
- threats of violence and murder
- violence against women
- body discovery and crime scene content
- brief corpse description and postmortem staging

THE RAIN HAS A MOUTH TONIGHT.

It speaks against the glass in long, wet syllables—tapping, sliding, pooling at the sill where the caulk has gone to rot.

The room smells of that rot: damp wood, the mineral shadow of old water. Underneath it, the cold vinegar tang of the window frame sweating in the draft.

Pressing my fingertip to the pane, I trace a droplet's path down, down, down to where it swells fat at the bottom and holds there, trembling, refusing to fall.

Remarkable, the stubbornness of small things.

She is sitting at the bus stop. Third bench from the left, beneath the fractured light that buzzes and spits its yellow glow in fitful, moth-drunk intervals. That sick electrical lull that belongs to dying things penetrates my ears. Not through the glass, or through the rain. No. I supply the sound myself. I have stood under that light a million times to know its song by heart.

That is what it means to pay attention. To truly see.

Her hair is so dark it drinks the rain, falling past her shoulders in damp ribbons she has not bothered to push from her face. A paperback rests open on her knee. She has not turned a page in four minutes.

I have counted.

I always count.

Every portrait needs a subject. I found mine on a Thursday. She is like a wren. Small, unassuming. A bird most people walk past without registering, or truly understanding that the ordinary is only so to people who have never learned how to look. I have spent considerable time learning how to look. In the end, it is the only skill that matters.

I used to watch birds from a different window, in a different city, when I was a different boy. The watching was the same. I went very still. I made myself invisible. I waited.

My little wren tugs the collar of her coat tighter. For one brief, luminous second, she glances up—not toward me, never toward me, they never look up—at the streetlight as if she can will it to behave. The glow catches her eyes.

Green.

They are not the pale, watered-down green of sea glass or hospital walls. This green is wet earth and crushed mint, the underside of a leaf, the second before the storm splits it from the branch.

My breath fogs the window. I wipe it clean with my sleeve. I don't want anything between us. Not yet.

She returns to her book. Crosses one ankle over the other. Pushes a strand of wet hair behind her ear with a patience that tells me she has done this a thousand times and will do it a thousand more—this quiet, ordinary ritual of waiting for a bus that runs twelve minutes late on Thursdays, because the city does not care about her, because no one on this street is paying attention to the exact shade of her eyelashes against her cheek or how her bottom lip catches between her teeth when she reads.

No one but me.

I imagine the taste of her fear. Not the act—I do not conjure the act, not yet—but the taste I allow myself to have. The moment her fear turns inside her, when understanding curdles and the body begins to leak its terror through every pore.

It will be copper at the root, salt at the edges. Beneath both, the bruised perfume of petals beginning to brown. I will not know its truest flavor until the hummingbird rhythm of her throat beats against the pad of my thumb in nauseated bursts, so fast it feels wrong, as if her body is trying to climb out through her skin and flee without her.

That is the moment I desire.

Panic will set in. The adrenal sweetness that rises off a body in the last minute—the one that cuts through every perfume a woman has ever put on her wrists—will flood the space between us until I can taste it on my teeth.

I will savor it.

Little wren's pupils will blow wide, those green irises swelling to a thin, trembling ring. In that exquisite contraction, she will *see* me. *Truly* see me. It will not be the face I wear at the grocery store. Or the polite nod I offer the neighbor when he fumbles with his keys in the hall.

No, she will be presented with the real architecture. The dark cathedral I have built behind my mask.

And she will be so beautiful in that seeing.

They always are.

The last breaths are the precious ones. Shallow, thinning, like a song winding down to its final note, each one more delicate than the last, all of them a gift she will not know she is giving. I will hold her gaze through every single one. I will not blink. I owe her that. I owe them all that.

After, my little wren will live inside me forever, pressed flat the same way she does that crease in her paperback with her thumb. Kept. Treasured. More loved in the keeping than she ever was in the living.

Is that not mercy?

My forehead meets the glass. It is cold. Good. The cold helps. The cold is a leash, and I am straining at the end of it, teeth bared, tongue thick against the roof of my mouth. I *need* her—

I peel myself off the window. My hands are shaking. I flex them, curl them into fists, release, curl them again. The knuckles pop one by one like wet twigs, the sound reverberating in the quiet. My breath has gone ragged, which I do not remember allowing. I can hear it hitting the back of my throat.

The apartment is dark. The television flickers from the other room. There are no sounds except the rain and me.

I can walk away from the glass. I can close the curtain, sit down, and eat the dinner I made two hours ago that's gone cold on the counter—plain chicken, white rice, a discipline I maintain because discipline is the fence that separates monsters like me from the ones who get caught. I can be good tonight. I have been good for weeks.

Weeks.

I turn away.

And the ceiling speaks.

It never starts loud. It always begins as a low, wet vibration I feel more than hear, settling into the base of my skull the way water finds a crack in a foundation. Evil purrs through my molars, prickling along the skin behind my ears.

I lift my eyes.

The stain is there, as it always is. Brown and spreading, a discolored bloom in the plaster directly above my chair. *Water damage,* I told the landlord once. *Old pipes.* He shrugged and said he'd get to it. He has not gotten to it. I never asked again. If he does, I will, most certainly, have to stall him.

It is shaped like a hand. I noticed that years ago, and I have tried very hard to unnotice it—the same way I try to unsee a face in the grout of bathroom tile, or the silhouette of something wrong in the gap beneath a door. Five fingers splayed wide, reaching. The thumb is darker than the rest, almost black at the center. When the light shifts, or when the television flits from blue to white in the next room, the hand appears to flex.

Come back to the window.

I do not dare to move.

Come back. Look at her. She's waiting for you.

The voice is not a voice. It is a force. A weight behind my left eye, a pressure at the nape of my neck, a taste of pennies dissolving on my tongue. It does not have a name. It does not need one. I know where it lives. Up there, behind the stain, in the dark wet space lodged behind the plaster and whatever else waits above it.

Where I keep my precious things.

"Not now. Not yet." My voice sounds foreign in this empty room. Thin. Human. Not me at all.

The stain darkens.

Green. She's got green eyes. You always loved green eyes. You remember how the color changed at the end, don't you? How it deepened right before it went still, like a pond freezing over.

My fists clench. I remember. Help me, I remember everything.

Go back to the window. Forever is so lonely, and the dark is so quiet. Keep her, as you keep me. You promised. I have been waiting—

"Stop!"

—for you to bring someone new.

The rain hammers the window. I am standing in the

middle of my apartment with my fists at my sides, jaw locked, muscles drawn bowstring-tight, iron and heat slithering down the back of my throat.

Above me, the stain is pulsing. Faintly. Rhythmically. In time with my heartbeat. Or my heartbeat in time with it. I have not been able to tell the difference in a very long time.

Just look. You don't have to do anything. Look at her one more time.

"It's always one more with you."

One more walk past her building to learn the cadence of her lights—which ones she kills first, which room she lingers in longest, whether she throws the deadbolt or only the knob.

One more, one more, one more, until the distance between looking and touching collapses like wet paper, then I am standing somewhere I should not be with something in my hands I cannot put down.

I cross the room.

I do not go to the window.

I go to the chair beneath the stain. I sit, tilt my head back until the crown of my skull rests against the cushion, and the hand on the ceiling fills the whole of my vision.

That sweet-wet rot floods my lungs. I stare at the brown bloom until the edges blur, until the fingers relax, until the pressure behind my eye dulls to a patient throb.

"Not tonight," I whisper.

The stain says nothing. It does not have to. We both know I will be at the window tomorrow. And the night after. And the night after that.

Patience, I seem to exhale.

A slow, damp sigh stirs the hair at my temple, though there is no draft in this room, no window open anywhere near me.

I've taught you that, haven't I?

Outside, the hydraulic sigh of the bus doors reaches

through the thin glass. My little wren will be standing now, folding her book closed, tucking it under her arm, climbing the steps with those green eyes pointed forward, going home to a life she does not know has an expiration date.

I close my eyes. Reopen them.

The stain spreads another inch. It feels as if someone steps into the room with me, bringing that displacement of silence and that small shift in the air.

Behind it, in the pitch dark, hidden deep, something that used to be a woman smiles.

Chapter One

ELIAS

FOUR MONTHS AGO, at his retirement party, my partner pulled me aside with a drink in his hand and said I was starting to look like one of our victims—hollow around the eyes, gone around the edges.

It's the kind of thing only a man walking out the door can say to the man staying behind. I laughed because the alternative was admitting he was right, and I wasn't ready to do that in a room full of people who still needed to believe I was holding it together.

Routine helps with that. Rules help more. And I haven't sat on a barstool since that night.

The four months between then and now have been crime scenes, cold coffee, and the depressing shade of gray this city turns when I've been reading autopsy reports longer than I've been sleeping.

Thankfully, the case board at the precinct hasn't moved in a week. My apartment is doing that thing where the walls shrink an inch every hour, and the silence I bring home has started to whir like a refrigerator left open in the dark.

So I drive.

Better the road than the apartment.

I end up at a place I've never been, some dive on the south side with a neon sign bleeding red into the rain-slicked sidewalk. The name doesn't register. That's the point.

The air inside hits in a slow, stale wave—spilled beer gone viscid in the floorboards, fryer grease from the kitchen, the sugary afterimage of somebody's vape, and under all of it the weak ammonia of a bar mat that needs changing.

My boots stick to the floor on the way to the counter. The stool I drop onto is cracked leather, patched with tape that's peeling at one corner and digging into the back of my thigh.

The drinks are cheap. The jukebox drowns out the ringing in my ears, but the low volume still lets me think. I order a martini in a tumbler because it's the drink that asks nothing of me.

I'm two in when I hear her laugh.

It doesn't belong here. It cuts through the muddy acoustics like a razor through smoke—bright, completely unbothered— and the sound turns my head before my brain gets a chance to explain why. Occupational hazard, I suppose. I notice things I'm not asked to notice. And I notice *her* before I realize that I am.

She's three stools down, leaning over the bar top with her chin propped on her fist, blonde hair falling around her face in a beautiful mess that took either zero effort or a lot of it. Cheeks pink from whatever sunset-colored drink she's had more than one of. Lips closed around the straw. Her shoulder is bare where her shirt has been losing a war with gravity all night, and there's a slip of something lace-edged underneath that she hasn't bothered to fix.

She starts telling the bartender a story with her hands. When she hits the punchline, her whole body vibrates with that same laugh, shoulders shaking, one heel kicking the bottom rung of her stool like a kid who can't sit still.

I drag my eyes back to my glass. The ice has melted into nothing. I drink it anyway because idle hands have always been a problem.

Doesn't work.

The woman's laugh finds me again, and I'm indexing everything before I can stop—left-handed, she cradles the glass with her dominant one. There's a small silver ring on her index finger, scratched on the inside of the band like she's had it a long time. Her chest bears a constellation of freckles that vanish beneath the slipped collar of her shirt. The little tendon that jumps in her wrist when she gestures. I could write her up in a report. I could describe her to a sketch artist from memory in six months. Some faces leave. Hers settles.

I don't realize I'm staring until she catches me.

Her eyes are blue. Deep, not the pale, washed-out blue of a morning sky. This is the blue of electricity held behind glass, backlit from the inside, too bright for the lighting in this room.

And she's amused. That's the part I wasn't ready for. Amused, like a wolf might be, pacing the edge of a clearing with no doubt about how this ends.

She picks up her drink and closes the gap between us. Her perfume reaches me before she does. Its warmth has nothing to do with temperature. Cloves and something darker underneath, smoky and a little sweet, like vanilla steeped in bourbon and the last breath of a fire gone to coals.

"You look like you're solving a crime." She slides onto the stool beside me. Not a polite one or two seats down. Nope, the one where her knee can brush mine if either of us swivels in the other's direction.

"Just drinking."

"Sure." She sets her glass down. The sunset concoction sweats against the wood in a pale ring. "But you were doing that thing where your eyes go narrow, and you tilt your head like you're reading fine print. Very Sherlock Holmes." She scrunches her nose. "It's either a crime or a crossword."

The corner of my mouth twitches. "You came over here to tell me that?"

"I came over here because you might be the most interesting person in this bar, and that includes the guy in the corner who's been arguing with a jukebox for twenty minutes."

There is, in fact, a man jabbing at a jukebox like he's defusing a bomb. A short laugh shoots out of me. Rough. Underused. The muscles in my jaw don't quite remember the feeling.

Her face lights up. "There's the proof."

"Of what?"

"That you're not actually made of stone." She sips her drink and watches me over the rim. "I was worried for a second."

"Stone is a strong word."

"Granite, then. Marble, if you want to be fancy about it."

Her elbow grazes mine on the bar. That sliver of skin is next to nothing, but the charge of it sparks straight into my molars.

Motioning to the bartender for another, I ask, "What's your story?"

Tilting her head, glossy lips part around a smile that the red neon bar sign turns filthy without her doing a thing to earn it. She tucks a blonde curl behind her ear, pretends to think, drawls the word "Hmm," and lets it hang. "I'm a woman of *many* mysteries."

Something old in me lifts its head.

"Let me see." She squints at the ceiling like she's consulting a teleprompter, only she can see. "I was born in a lighthouse during a thunderstorm. My mother was a runaway contortionist. My father—retired jewel thief. Very debonair. Terrible cook." She holds up a finger. "I was raised by a collective of morally flexible circus performers who taught me the art of deception, fire-eating, and"—a pause, a beat held for effect—"escaping handcuffs."

I stare at her while the bartender slides a fresh drink in front of me.

She takes a sip, then continues with a face so serious it could pass a polygraph. "Now I'm here. Blending into society. Planning my triumphant return to the glamorous world of illicit crime and trapeze work." She leans in, voice dropping to a conspiratorial hush that puts her mouth inches from my ear. Her breath is warm. Sugar, vodka, and a hint of peach underneath. "The trapeze is the harder part, honestly. Upper body strength is no joke."

My laugh comes out as a startled, stupid sound I don't recognize.

She smiles like she's won something.

Maybe she has.

"Why do I feel as though you've rehearsed that for a crowd?" I swirl my glass in a lazy circle. The ice knocks gently against the rim.

"Maybe." She hooks one foot on the rung of my stool and closes another inch between us. The toe of her shoe rests against the inside of my calf. Neither of us acknowledges it. "But *you're* the first one I've deemed worthy of the full performance." She winks.

It should be ridiculous. For reasons unknown to me, it isn't.

"I'm honored."

"You should be. The abridged version doesn't include the handcuffs."

I exhale through my nose. Half of it, a laugh, the rest a concession. This is the part where I should be pulling back. *This* is where the version of me that's been living in crime scenes for years should be doing the math—*stranger, bar, no name, this is not how you do it*—and excusing himself to the men's room and never coming back.

I do the math.

I stay.

By the time a line feels crossed, I've usually been standing on the other side of it for a while.

The bar around us thickens. Bodies push past, a burly man behind me shouts a drink order, the bassline through the floorboards streams up into the soles of my boots. I register all of it at the edge of my hearing, filed and dismissed. The center of the room is her. She makes the rest of it set dressing.

There's ink smudged along the side of her hand, as if she wrote something down in a hurry before she came out tonight. The detail lodges itself inside my mind with the others.

She nudges my shoulder with hers. "Your turn."

"Not until you tell me your name."

She regards me for a long moment. Chin tilted. Lips curved. Eyes doing that thing where they see straight through the walls I've built and look politely amused by the view.

"Hmm." Her teeth catch her bottom lip. I feel it somewhere I shouldn't. "Earn it."

"How?"

"Story first. Name after."

"Harsh terms."

"I'm a harsh woman."

I take a drink to buy time. The vodka heats against my tongue. "Mine's less entertaining."

Heat rises off her skin in a wave, bringing cloves and leather with it. She props her chin on her hand. "Try me."

"All right."

Her eyes flare with curiosity, and the sight catches at a place in me I prefer left undisturbed. She's completely carefree, and whatever she's guessed lives behind my silence, hasn't made her cautious.

I turn toward her on the stool. My knee finds hers under the bar. "I'm a guy who sees the worst thing that's ever happened to someone. Then I reduce it to paperwork."

The playfulness in her face doesn't leave. It deepens. Like she turned the page and found the chapter she actually came for. "I knew it. Cop?"

"Detective."

"Homicide?"

"What makes you say that?"

She traces the rim of her glass with one finger. "You've got that look. You're always half somewhere else." She meets my eyes. "Somewhere no one should have to go alone."

The room thins. The noise behind her flattens out to a far-off roar, and what she just said slides under a rib like a blade slipped between the bones. I've known this woman for half an hour, and she recognized something most people spend years politely avoiding.

"Name."

She shakes her head. Smiles. "Earn it."

"I gave you my dark, tragic backstory."

"You gave me two sentences. I gave you a whole circus." She lifts her glass. "Buy me another one of these, and we'll call it progress."

I'm already signaling the bartender.

"You are *definitely* the most interesting person here." That laugh slips under my skin again and makes itself at home, while her knee nudges mine under the bar again.

The night bends around us. One drink becomes two. Two becomes a conversation that doesn't care what time it is. She tells me she's a Scorpio, like it's a warning. I tell her I don't believe in astrology. She gasps so loud the bartender looks over.

She asks what the worst part of my job is. I say the paperwork, and her eyes narrow, telling me she knows I'm lying and is letting me have it anyway.

I ask her what she does. She says it depends on the night, with a grin that could start a war.

At that point, I stop trying to figure her out. I let myself be in her orbit instead. Figuring things out implies distance. I'm past that.

I watch the trajectory of her hands when she talks, listen to how her laugh changes when something I've said is drier than I meant, the increments by which she leans in, testing how close she can get before I pull back.

I never, not once, pull back.

Around the third drink, she steals the olive from my glass and eats it without breaking eye contact, tongue catching a drop of brine from the tip of her thumb. I feel that somewhere entirely unrelated to my thumb.

On the fourth, her hand finds my thigh. Casual. A dare disguised as a landing. She leaves it there while telling me about the time she accidentally set off a fire alarm at a hotel in Savannah.

I'm not listening to the story. I'm cataloging the warmth of every finger through the denim of my jeans.

"You're not paying attention."

"I'm paying attention to everything. Trust me, that ability rarely behaves like a gift."

The teasing drops out of her face for a beat, and underneath it, a raw, unguarded flash of want strips the charm off the room.

She recovers, smiles slow. "Everything?"

I nod.

"Prove it."

I lean back against the barstool. "You're left-handed." With my thumb stroking over the rim of my glass, my eyes roam over the length of her. "You pull your bottom lip between your teeth when you know what you're about to say is going to strike. You say things for effect. You've touched me eleven times since you sat down, and every single one was calculated and on purpose. Your pulse just jumped at your throat when I said that." I hold her gaze. "And you've been clenching your thighs together so hard the seam of those jeans is rubbing right where you want my mouth."

Her throat works. I watch the swallow travel down the line of her neck. The flush spreads beneath her collarbones in a slow, rising tide.

"That," she starts, voice gone a little rough, "is either the sexiest or the most terrifying thing anyone's ever said to me."

"Which one?"

"I haven't decided." Her fingers tighten on my thigh. I have my answer. Want is easiest to recognize in the body. Harder to mistake.

A tipsy woman bumps her stool from behind, pushing her forward. Her free hand catches flat on my chest to steady herself, and the bar dissolves—the noise, the bodies, the neon in the window—all of it collapses to one bright, small point.

Her perfume floods the inch between us. Dark and ruinous and close enough to breathe.

She doesn't pull back. I'm not sure I'd let her if she tried.

"I don't even know your name," I say, barely above the music.

She looks at my mouth. Takes her time about it. "You won't need it."

Her hand curls around mine, and the last civilized thought swirling in my brain is:

This is absurd. I should know better.

But it all comes apart the second she hauls me off the stool and leads us toward the door.

The rain hits us in a cold silver shock. The smell of wet asphalt and the exhaust of a car that just pulled away drift through the air.

I gesture in the direction of my truck. She doesn't let go of my hand as we wind through the parking lot, all the way there.

Chapter Two

ROWAN

ONE MONTH LATER...

He's been coming here for weeks.

My stranger.

I don't know his name. I don't know his voice or what he does when the sun is up, and the rest of the world pretends to be decent. All I have is a silhouette leaning against the far wall of The Midnight Hour like the building was poured around him, arms crossed, jaw set, dark eyes pinned to me with a patience that borders on terrifying.

The other men in this room are noise. Drunk breath and grabby fingers and dollar bills held out like dog treats. They blur after a while, all slack mouths and sweaty palms and the same cheap delusion that a twenty-fold lengthwise buys them a piece of me.

The stranger in the shadows never tips.

Never approaches the stage.

Never flags me down for a private or slips a folded napkin to the bartender with a phone number and a wink like the regulars who think whiskey on the rocks is a love language.

He just watches.

And I let him.

Which probably says something unflattering about me. I'm not in the mood to translate it. I've never been one of those women who go cold in the face of danger. Fear doesn't deaden me. It strips me down to the nerve. Lights me up when the air goes dull, when a room turns wrong, when a mysterious man looks like he might be trouble.

I'm not like the nice girls who see danger and back away. No, I feel my pulse turn molten, and every dark hallway in my body wakes up all at once.

Maybe it's damage. Maybe it's some busted survival instinct that learned a long time ago to turn panic into hunger because hunger feels better than helplessness. Whatever it is, danger has always had a way of making my body burn brighter, hotter, more awake. Like if ruin is already standing in the doorway, I'd rather drag it close enough to kiss than let it watch me shake.

The club smells the same as it always does. Sweaty, cologne gone sour, hairspray, the sticky sugary leftovers of spilled cocktails, the burnt-plastic sweetness of a fog machine working overtime in the rafters.

Under all of it, the chemical bite of the floor cleaner the day shift uses, and they never quite get it right. I know these smells the way I know my own pulse. It used to turn my stomach. Now it means *work*.

The bass lives in the atmosphere, crawling up through the platform, through the soles of my thigh-highs, through the bones of my shins, and settling deep in my belly where it belongs.

Wrapping my hand around the pole, the chrome shocks cold against my palm for one breath before it heats. The first beat drops. My body answers before my brain does.

I find him immediately.

Same corner.

Same shadow.

But tonight is different. Tonight, I catch a glimpse of his face.

The strobes cut just right, or maybe he moved half an inch forward, because for the first time, the light grazes the line of his jaw, the curve beneath his cheekbone, the dark slash of brows over eyes I can finally confirm are watching *me* and not the other blonde two stages over.

Me.

Only me.

That should feel like a warning. Instead, it lands like a hand at the base of my spine.

That makes my hot, reckless heart crack open in my chest, and my mind slide backward one month, to a bar I can't remember the name of, and a man I can't forget the hands of.

I tell myself it isn't him. It *can't* be. The stranger in the corner has a stillness my cop never had, or maybe I just never saw him still.

My cop was restless energy, barely leashed behind a badge and whatever lived under it, clenched so tight he looked like he could crack his own teeth. *This* man is steel. He's been holding himself in that exact pose for two weeks and has never once changed his position.

Not him. Not possible.

But under the strobes, with the red and violet light slicing his face into pieces, I pretend it is.

I want you to fuck me right here. Where anyone could see.

The memory is physical before it's anything else. The cold press of the passenger window against my temple, fogged where my breath hit the glass. The bite of the seatbelt buckle was digging into the small of my back, where he'd pinned me. I still have a mark there, a pale half-moon I catch in the mirror after a shower.

The taste of him on my tongue, vodka and something smoky, I never figured out. His palm was wide over my thigh, calluses at the base of each finger, ones he got from a grip he uses every day. A cop's hands. A man who pulls a trigger, racks a slide, writes a report, then goes home and does not sleep much.

And he fucked me inside the cab of his truck like he'd been thinking about it since the second I sat down beside him. Maybe he had. I know I had.

I let him. I more than let him. I yanked him closer, fisted the front of his shirt, and dared him with my mouth before he had his belt undone.

It was filthy. And wrong. A thing I haven't dared to tell any friends about because my voice would soften and give away how much I liked it.

His hands pinned my thighs apart. He railed me like he had something to prove, and I took each achingly delicious inch of it with my head tipped back and my nails gouging into his neck while the bass from the bar bled through the parking lot surrounding us.

Christ, the way you grip me when I hit that spot. Do it again. Let me hear you.

I came so hard I couldn't see. He buried his groan in my throat and held me there—suspended, fucked, shaking, until the world found its balance again.

One of the most pleasant mistakes I've ever made with a man whose name I never asked for.

The rest is a flicker I don't allow myself to linger on, because I have a song to finish, a body to run, and a paycheck to earn. But that one image of his hand at my throat, and my voice breaking on a sound I'd never made before, never stops playing on repeat.

My eyes glide back to the shadow lurking in the corner.

Tonight, under the lights, with his eyes locked on me like I'm the only thing in this room taking a breath—

I pretend.

Wrapping my thigh around the pole, I slide, slow, controlled, the metal forcing a cold line between my breasts as I descend. My back arches, hair sweeping the stage floor. I hold the inversion until the burn in my core takes over. His attention hooks onto me.

The room fades. The jeers, the whoops, the DJ's bored voice between songs, all of it peels back. There is the pole. There is the beat. There is only the shadow.

I climb. Muscles coil. At the apex, I hook my knee, and my body unfurls like a ribbon coming undone—arms open, spine curved, throat exposed. An offering to the man who won't come close enough to accept it.

Story of my life, honestly.

When I right myself and sway my hips into the next transition, I stop pretending this is a routine, acting like the arch of my back and the slow grind of my body against the pole is for the room.

It's for him.

Every.

Deliberate.

Movement.

My fingers trail down my throat, over my collarbone, trace the edge of my bra—a little tease on whether I'm keeping it on tonight. The crowd at the rail cheers. A fresh flutter of bills drifts onto the stage. I don't register a single one of them. Because he's moved. Arms uncrossed now, one hand braced flat against the wall behind him. From here, the tension strung through his shoulders looks like a wire about to snap.

Good. I want him wound tight. I want him tense and fighting it.

Sinking into a deep body weave against the pole, the metal slides between my thighs. The friction sends a lush ache radiating up into my pussy that has nothing to do with performance. My fingers find my nipples through the thin fabric of my bra, and I pinch, not the theatrical little taunt the customers eat up, but hard, real, *for me.*

The tremor that kicks through me is truthful. My lips part on a moan I didn't plan. I don't fake the sound. If anything, I grind harder against the pole. The pressure builds. My gaze locks on his corner. The world could be on fire, and I wouldn't blink.

He doesn't move. Or turn away.

That's the part that gets me wound up.

That refusal—that absolute stillness—while I come undone twenty feet from him, is the most obscene thing anyone has ever done to me in this club.

The men at the rail think they're getting a show. They have no idea. What they're watching is a conversation they can't hear, broadcast on a frequency only two people in this room are tuned to.

I drag my nails down my ribs. I'm soaking wet. My hips drag one last time over the chrome, surely leaving my mess behind.

I let the last beat devour me whole.

Lights sweep over the area with a hard blue wash for the next girl's intro, and the scent of the fog machine thickens for a moment, catching at the back of my throat.

My legs shake on my way down the stage steps. The applause and whistles behind me are static, crawling across every exposed inch of me. A man in the front yells something I don't catch and don't want to.

I look up, breathless, skin buzzing, pulse a thick drumbeat between my legs—

He's gone.

The corner is empty. Wall, shadow, and the echo of his touch clinging to my skin.

My stomach drops with a disappointment so irrational and so scraped out, I'm ashamed of it before it finishes settling. I shouldn't care. That's probably the most embarrassing part. He's a stranger who haunts a strip club. That's not a love story. That's a restraining order in the making.

And yet.

That little bird in my throat is still singing: *I know you.*

I tell it to shut up.

Dev, the head bouncer here, waits at the edge of the stage and nods at me. For a second, I want to grab the sleeve of his shirt and say, *"Did you see him? Did you see where he went? Did he come in through the front or the side?"*

And I don't, because I already know how that sentence sounds out loud.

I yank the curtain into the dressing room. The smell changes in an instant—baby powder, setting spray, the sour-sweet reek of a mini-fridge that should have been cleaned last week, Rayen's vanilla body lotion. Dove is crying in the corner into her phone. Syn is microwaving popcorn.

The mirror is ringed in white bulbs, half of them burned out. I fall into the chair and rake both hands through my hair, gripping at the roots until my scalp stings.

The curtain jerks open before I can spiral any further. Devon fills the doorway with his usual brick-wall energy, one forearm braced against the frame, brows pulled low enough to mean business. In the dressing-room light, he looks bigger, black tee stretched across his shoulders, radio clipped to his belt, eerie silver eyes seething.

"Ro."

I drop my hands from my hair. "Hi, Dev."

"Don't hi, Dev me." His gaze sweeps over me, quick and efficient, making sure I'm intact before it hardens. "What the hell was that out there?"

Dove is still crying in the corner. Syn is digging burnt popcorn out of the microwave with a plastic fork. Neither of them bothers pretending not to listen.

I lean back in the chair and cross one leg over the other like I've got all the time in the world. "You're gonna have to be more specific. I do a lot of questionable things for money in this building."

Devon's mouth twitches, but only for a second. "Cute." He steps inside and lets the curtain fall shut behind him. "I mean the part where you sexually assaulted the pole."

That pulls a laugh out of me. "Wow. Poetry."

"Ro." His voice loses the edge of humor, and there it is, the thing that makes Devon Devon. He can bark like a bouncer all night long, but underneath that gruff, he's still the guy who keeps extra phone chargers behind the bar for the girls and walks us to our cars when the lot feels sketchy.

I sigh and let my head tip back. "I don't know."

"Bullshit."

"Language," I murmur.

He folds his arms. "You literally work in a strip club."

"Still. You're in a lady's dressing room."

That almost gets another smile out of him. He studies me for a beat too long, and his expression morphs, frustration giving way to something narrower. More careful.

"It was him again?" he asks.

I don't answer right away, which is answer enough.

Devon exhales through his nose. "Shadow guy."

I make a face. "That is such a serial-killer nickname."

"Yeah, because he gives serial-killer vibes, Rowan."

"He does not."

Devon scowls at me.

"Okay," I say. "He does a little."

"A little?" He pushes off the doorframe and plants his hands on his hips. "The man stands in the same corner every week, like he pays rent there. Never buys a drink. Never tips. Never talks. Just stares at you like he's trying to memorize your dental records."

A laugh cracks out of me. "My dental records?"

"You know what I mean."

"I do." I fiddle with the strap of my boot, not looking at him. "And for the record, he does not stare at my teeth."

The silence that follows is heavy. When I glance up, Devon is staring like I've walked barefoot into traffic.

"Oh, no," he says slowly. "Absolutely not."

"What?"

"Obviously, you're into it."

I open my mouth to deny it, then close it again because apparently tonight I'm committed to making his point for him.

Devon drags a hand down his face. "Jesus Christ, Ro."

"Do not Jesus-Christ me."

"I will Jesus-Christ you all I want. Not five minutes ago, I watched you have a full-body religious experience onstage over a man whose entire personality is 'corner.'"

Despite myself, I snort.

Devon points at me. "And that right there is how you get murdered."

"That feels dramatic."

"That feels accurate." He drops his hand and widens his stance, broad shoulders bunching under his shirt. "You don't know anything about this guy."

"I know he watches."

"Yeah, that's the part I'm not loving."

I look down at my hands. Glitter clings to my knuckles. My

pulse is all over the place, acting like I'm still under the lights. "I know."

Devon's voice softens. "Then what was that?"

That.

The question hangs there, heavier than I want it to be. I could lie. Shrug it off. Make it a joke and save us both the trouble. But Devon's been catching me when I fall apart in one form or another for two years now, and lying to him has always felt a little like kicking a puppy.

So I pick at a loose thread on my skirt and say, "He reminds me of someone."

Devon goes still. "What someone?"

I hesitate. "This guy."

His eyes narrow. "What guy?"

Heat climbs my face, which is ridiculous. I've danced half-naked in front of three dozen strangers tonight, and this is what's embarrassing me.

I shrug. "A guy."

"Ro."

"Oh my God, don't dad-voice me."

"Then stop talking like a teenager sneaking in past curfew."

I press my lips together, then blow out a breath. "I met someone a month ago."

Devon's expression changes so subtly that another person might miss it. I don't. The hard line of his mouth goes harder. His jaw sets. Not enough to make a scene. But enough to let me know the information stuck somewhere tender.

"A month ago," he repeats.

"It was one night."

He laughs once, humorless. "Of course it was."

I lift one shoulder. "I didn't get his name."

Devon stares. Then he looks up at the ceiling like he's asking the universe for patience and not getting any.

"You had sex with a stranger whose name you do not know," he says flatly.

"When you say it like that, it sounds irresponsible."

He drops his gaze back to me. "It is irresponsible."

"Thank you for that groundbreaking insight."

He ignores me. "And now you think Creeper in the Corner is him?"

"I don't know." My voice comes out smaller than I mean it to. "Maybe. Or maybe I want him to be."

That shuts him up. For half a second, the room loses some of its noise. The microwave goes silent, popcorn finally surrendering in the background.

There's an emotion etched on Devon's face that I can't quite read at first. Then I do, and it makes an awkward, unwelcome feeling twist in my stomach.

It's jealousy. Not the ugly, risk-our-friendship kind. He's not possessive. Just there, when I need him. And when I don't. Like a protective older brother. More in my eyes than his.

A brief shadow of the emotion is crossing a decent man's face because some faceless idiot in a dark corner got something from me he's never had. But has always wanted.

He covers it fast, but not fast enough.

"So that whole thing on stage," he says, voice careful now, "was for one-night stand guy."

I stare at a sequin on my thigh. "That is the worst possible name for him."

"Am I wrong?"

"No," I mutter.

Devon huffs out a laugh and shakes his head. "Unbelievable."

"What?"

"You." He points at me again, but there's no fire in it now. Only affection and exasperation braided together so tight they're basically the same thing. "You've got half this city throwing money at you, and you go full feral over a man who might not even be the right man."

I smile despite myself. "I contain multitudes."

"You contain bad ideas."

"Also true."

His mouth finally gives, curving at one corner. Then his eyes flick toward the curtain, the club beyond it, and his face goes guarded again. "You tell me if he comes near you."

"He hasn't done anything."

"He's been breathing in your direction for weeks. That counts."

Standing, I smooth my hands down my sides. "You're ridiculous."

"And you're trouble."

"That feels rich coming from a man who once head-butted a customer into a jukebox for calling Rayen babygirl."

"He had it coming."

"He did."

Devon steps back and lifts the curtain for me, then pauses before I pass him. "If he is your one-night stand guy, and he makes you do that on stage again, I'm gonna need his name."

I look up at him. "Why?"

His throat works. "So I know who to fuck up properly."

That makes me laugh for real, bright enough that Dove looks up from her phone and rolls her eyes.

Devon's hard edges soften at the sound for a second. Then he jerks his head toward the hall. "Come on. You've got two songs before Velvet's set ends, and if you try to mope in here all night, I'm telling Syn to hide your lashes."

"You wouldn't dare."

"Try me." He holds the curtain open. I brush past him, shoulder knocking his arm on purpose.

And because he's Devon, and because he's impossible, and has apparently decided I'm his favorite pain in the ass, he mutters under his breath as I pass, "Pick a guy who doesn't look like he has bodies in his basement next time."

I grin over my shoulder. "No promises."

Devon groans, and I head out to make my rounds with my pulse still skipping and his concern hot between my shoulder blades.

Chapter Three

ELIAS

THE DEAD WOMAN on the floor isn't what stops me.

The photograph is.

The apartment smells the same as they all do after: copper turning brown in the air, the chemical snap of luminol someone sprayed in the hall, and underneath both, the ordinary scent of the woman who lived here.

Dish soap.

A candle that burned down to the wick on the kitchen counter, its wax pooled into a cold white lake.

The papery smell of old books. She was a reader. The shelves along the far wall are full of them, spines cracked with use, a few stacked on the floor beside a pair of slippers she'll never step back into.

I notice that. I always notice the small things, the ones no one else in the room is counting.

I kneel beside the dining table, nitrile gloves creaking as I turn the glossy print face-up. The room works around me in its usual crime-scene rhythm. Radio chatter, CSU shutters clicking in the bedroom, the metallic buzz of the overhead light that needs a new ballast, the scuff of paper booties on hardwood.

All of it dulls the moment *her* face comes into view.

I don't mean the dead woman's.

In the picture, a woman sleeps on her side, one arm folded beneath a white pillow, blonde hair spilling in soft waves across her cheek. An ordinary headboard behind her. The sheet twisted around her hips in a way that says she turned over moments before the shutter opened. Her bare shoulder glows in the wash of a streetlamp bleeding through half-open curtains. Her mouth is slightly parted, showing the smallest edge of her bottom lip.

She is vulnerable. Unaware. And someone wanted it documented.

I know her.

The recognition doesn't arrive as a thought. It's a hand around my throat—sudden, airless, total control.

My pulse drops hard into the bottom of my chest and sits there, thudding against the bone it shouldn't be touching.

I know that shoulder. The freckles scattered across it, the same ones I traced with my thumb in the dark.

I know the curve of that bottom lip because I bit it in the cab of my truck a month ago while the rain hammered the roof and the windows fogged so thick the parking lot disappeared from sight.

The memory surfaces before I'm able to push it aside.

The bass from the bar was still audible across the lot, thumping through my truck's frame as a second heartbeat. She'd climbed in first, pulled me after her by the front of my shirt. The dome light came on and caught her face, flushed, laughing, rain-wet, and I'd reached up to kill it because I wanted her in the dark where all other senses sharpen.

"You sure about this?" My mouth was right against her ear, one hand already snaking under the hem of her shirt, the other sliding up her thigh.

She answered with her mouth on my throat, fingers working my belt, and a sound I still hear some nights when I'm trying to sleep.

I got her jeans open before she finished with mine. She laughed, breathless, surprised, and the sound vibrated against my throat where her mouth was still working.

"Impatient," she whispered. I wasn't. I was already gone.

The seatbelt buckle bit into the small of her back. I felt it dig into my knuckle when I pinned her, and she gasped—a little pain and a whole lot of want. She rose up into me instead of away. The truck smelled of rain on hot vinyl and also her perfume, that dark clove-and-smoky leather scent, and the tang of sweat between us as the windows went white.

I dropped to my knees on the floorboard, hooked her thigh over my shoulder, and put my mouth on her before she could blink. One long, flat drag of my tongue from bottom to top, and the sound she made has been lodged inside my skull ever since.

She walked away afterward. No name. No number. No backward glance. Only the click of the passenger door and her silhouette disappearing into the rain while my engine idled, and my hands shook on the wheel.

I told myself it didn't matter. One night. Easy to forget.

I have never been a convincing liar. Because I found her again.

Two weeks after that night, a noise complaint took me to a club on the south side called The Midnight Hour. I saw her on the stage. Blonde hair. Same silver ring catching the light.

I denied it at first. It couldn't be her. I told myself it was coincidence before I let myself call it recognition.

She moved with graceful strength, and once she curved her spine around the pole, I knew. Similar to how one recognizes a voice before placing the face. Or how a scent hits and catapults you back in a room you left years ago.

I stood in the corner and didn't approach.

I went back the next week. Told myself I was checking in. Making sure the noise complaint was resolved. A lie so thin I could see through it before it finished forming.

Then I went back again. And again.

I never tipped. Never flagged her down. Never stepped out of the shadow at the far wall. I stood there with my arms crossed, watching her dance, and told myself that watching was harmless, that distance was the same thing as restraint, and that a man who doesn't close the gap is *still* a decent man.

I should have walked up to her. Asked her name. Proved I was only a man in a room.

I never found the right moment. That's the lie I told myself, anyway.

So, I kept going back. Holding my position. Drawing the line and staying behind it. Telling myself one more night won't hurt.

The photograph trembles in my hand. My glove creaks against the glossy paper. I'm gripping it too hard. A tech is going to notice. The M.E. is going to notice. I need to drop this where other pieces of evidence live, behind the glass wall I've spent a decade building between what I feel and what I show.

I force my fingers to ease. No one in the room needs to know I've stopped breathing.

Her face stares up at me from the print. Asleep. Unaware that a monster stood over her bed, watching her breathe, pressed the shutter. She never heard it. Never woke.

I check the back. Pure white. Zero lab markings.

I swept the rest of the apartment with CSU earlier. The victim doesn't have picture frames anywhere. No photo albums. Just the books on the shelves, a few unopened puzzles on the coffee table, and a life arranged with meticulous order.

The monster who placed this photograph did it with intent. Selected it. Carried it in. Set it facedown next to the victim, after the body was arranged, knowing that the first detective to kneel here would flip it over and find her.

Her.

"Ward." The medical examiner's voice cuts through the noise in my head. I'm still staring at the photograph when he adds, "Are you with me or the ghosts?"

"I don't have ghosts," I answer automatically. Ghosts would be easier. "Only questions."

"You getting anything off that?"

"Working on it." I rise and cross to the body.

She's on her back on the hardwood, posed beneath the chandelier with her arms at her sides and her head angled toward the entryway as though she's been arranged to greet whoever walks in.

Mid-twenties. Dark brown hair fanned out beneath her. It's too even and deliberate. Someone spread it with their fingers after she stopped moving. A white silk blouse torn open. Her lipstick is smeared across her chin in a streak that follows the direction of a hand, not a struggle.

Her eyes are open.

Green. Deep, dark green.

My stomach churns. I gulp down the taste of bile at the back of my throat and take inventory of every feature she possesses.

She's small. Narrow wrists. Bird-boned frame. The delicate line of her collar beneath the torn silk. She's a woman most people probably walked past without noticing. Nothing remarkable to anyone who wasn't paying close attention.

While the M.E. takes notes, I scan the room.

A half-empty mug of tea sits on the end table closest to the couch, a chamomile tag still draped over the rim. She'd been having a quiet night. Reading, probably. Drinking her tea. Waiting for nothing in particular.

The tea gets to me. Hours ago, she warmed her hands around it. Now it's going cold six feet from her body, and she will never pick it up again.

I make myself see her the same as any victim. Entirely. Systematically. Noting the bruising at her throat—bilateral, symmetrical, consistent with manual strangulation from the front. The positioning of the arms. The deliberate arrangement of the hair. The angle of her jaw. This was not fast. This was not rage.

This was patient.

"Who found her?"

A patrol officer leans in from the doorway. "Neighbor heard a scream around nine. Said it cut off fast. Saw someone in a hooded jacket leaving through the back stairwell, called it in. No good look at the face."

"Cameras?"

"Nothing. One out front's been spray-painted over. The other's been dead for months. Landlord says he put in a ticket."

A humorless sound grinds out of me. This city bleeds excuses.

The CSU photographer steps closer. "Ready to bag the photo?"

"In a second." I bring the photograph up again. Study the edges. Through the half-open curtains behind her sleeping form, I make out the distorted shape of an adjacent high-rise building. A sodium streetlamp casts a familiar yellow haze. The slip in the curtains shows nothing of the street. I can't make out any neighboring windows. Or landmarks. Just her. She *is* the landscape.

She was framed that way for a purpose.

The silver ring on her index finger catches the lamplight in the photograph. The same ring I clocked the night she sat down beside me at the bar. The same ring that flashed under the strobes at The Midnight Hour two nights ago, while I stood in the dark, watching her get herself off twenty feet away from me, like she was having a private conversation with my shadow.

I slide the photo into an evidence sleeve with steady hands. They're always steady. That is the fence I maintain.

"Log it as victim-related for now," the M.E. says, straightening, snapping off his gloves. "We'll confirm her ID once we—"

"She's not victim-related." My voice comes out flat and controlled. A door shut carefully instead of slammed. "She's a separate target."

The room goes silent.

"Whoever did this—" I look down at the body on the floor, the green eyes gone fixed and dull, the dark hair spread with careful fingers, the cold tea on the end table. "—wanted us to find *her*." I nod toward the evidence sleeve. "More than the woman he killed."

The CSU tech's voice is careful. "You're thinking there's a second victim?"

"I'm thinking we're looking at his next one."

I tuck the evidence sleeve under my arm. The glossy surface pushes against my ribs through the thin fabric of my shirt. Its weight is crushing, all the way to the bone.

"The one he hasn't broken yet."

Chapter Four

THE PHOTOGRAPHER

SHE LEFT her light on again.

Third window from the left, four floors up, the one with the secondhand curtains she bought on Ninth because she liked how the morning comes through them. I know this because I was there the morning after she hung them, watching the light do exactly what she hoped it would, spilling through the weave in long strips across her bedroom floor while she stood in the doorway with her coffee and smiled at the small private victory of a thing chosen well.

She smiles like that when no one is watching.

That is when she is most herself.

The rain has found its voice again tonight. It speaks against the pavement in long wet syllables, same as the first night I stood on this corner and understood what I was looking at.

Not a woman in a window, but a *conclusion*. The end of a question I have been asking in the dark for longer than I can remember.

She is the answer the universe composed while I was still learning to read the question, which is to say she arrived before I was ready for her. Fate is funny like that. She's been waiting for me without knowing. But some things are simply *inevitable*.

I have made my peace with inevitable things.

The stain taught me that.

I do not look at ceilings for the same reason you are not supposed to look at the sun. Not because looking is forbidden, but because I understand what looking costs, and I have learned to spend myself carefully.

But here, on this corner, in the rain, with the light of her window burning four floors above like a simmering coal jammed into the dark face of the building, that low, wet vibration behind my left eye blooms. Next is the pressure at the nape of my neck. Followed by the taste of pennies, patient and familiar on my tongue.

You're close, it says.

Yes.

How close?

Close enough to count her heartbeats if the window were open. Close enough to smell the earthy candle she burns in the evenings when she's trying to convince herself the apartment is a home and not a room she returns to.

The distance between standing here and standing there has become, in my more honest moments, a question of *when* rather than *whether*.

I've been honest with myself for a very long time.

The window light shifts. Her shadow moves across the curtain. I've memorized her silhouette exactly how cartographers memorize coastlines, inlets, and promontory archives, comprehending the precise geography of the very thing you intend to know completely.

She is changing. Or moving through the room on some small domestic errand—an errand that will mean nothing to the world and everything to me.

She is refilling a water glass, checking a lock, moving

through the sacred ordinary machinery of a life lived in beautiful ignorance of being watched.

I reach into my coat pocket.

The photograph is there. I have carried it for nine days now, the glossy surface worn soft at the edges from being kept close to my body, reshaped by contact, like a stone in a pocket becoming different from one left in a field.

It is not hers. I want to be precise about that because precision matters. Imprecision is the enemy of the work, and a man who cannot distinguish between what *is* and what *will be* is a man who confuses the map for the territory and gets lost in the dark between them.

I have never been lost.

This photograph is of the next subject. A series requires more than one sitting. The next movement in the composition. A woman with auburn hair spread across a pink pillow, one arm folded beneath her cheek, the city light catching the small gold watch she never takes off, even in sleep.

I stood over her bed for fourteen minutes on Tuesday. She never stirred. Her breathing was deep and even. She was entirely unaware of the gift I was giving her—the gift of being seen, chosen, and deemed worthy of the careful, patient attention most people move through their entire lives without ever receiving.

She will understand, eventually.

They always do.

This is the system. This is how I have always written it, the framework that the stain revealed to me in the dark, the wet forbearance of its teaching. One should never arrive at a crime scene empty-handed. I arrive with the *next* thing.

I place it carefully, face down, centered, a promise made in the dialect of glossy paper and stolen light, so that whoever comes after her, and whoever kneels beside the arranged body, turns the photograph over with their gloved hands—understands immediately that this is not an ending.

It is a *movement.*

A portrait series is never just one image. The work is not finished until the last frame. After all, the audience never realizes what they're witnessing until the final act.

My goldfinch's shadow crosses the curtain again, and the wet patient thing in my chest opens its eyes and breathes.

She is the current movement.

The one I have been moving toward since the night I watched her three blocks east, walking home under streetlights that buzz and spit their gold glow in fitful intervals. She looked up at the moon, and the glow caught her eyes for one suspended, radiant second.

Blue.

Not the cold blue of a shallow winter puddle. This was a storm held barely in check, all voltage and promise.

I have not recovered.

I did not recover from the wren at the bus stop either, which is how I know the pattern now. Recovery is not the point and never was. One is not meant to recover from the things that alter their framework. We are meant to carry them. *Keep* them. Hide them inside the part of us that holds precious things and understand that this is what we were built for.

The wren lives inside me now. She has been there since the last breath, when the green deepened and went still, then became a mirror and a surface that held the sky. She is kept. Treasured. More loved in the keeping than she ever was in the living.

My goldfinch in the window will understand this also.

Soon.

The woman with the auburn hair—my scarlet tanager—and the gold watch who sleeps so deeply on Tuesday nights will go to the pillow of my goldfinch's bed like goldfinch went to my little wren, and my wren went to the bed of the silver-eyed girl before her—the one with the paintings she will never finish and the dinner that went cold six feet from her body and the slippers she will never step back into. *Flycatcher.*

My signature is a promise. A note passed forward in the dark that says...

I am coming.

I have been standing at this corner for weeks, measuring the space between wanting and having with an accuracy that would astonish the people who think they know about patience. They do not. Patience is not waiting. Patience is knowing the exact moment and holding that knowledge in your body the same way you hold your breath underwater, feeling the pressure build, letting the burn begin, and welcoming the exquisite suffering, understanding it is nearly time.

Nearly.

The city moves around me as cities always do—oblivious, purposeful, the great indifferent machinery of a place that has never once looked down at what walks its streets. A cab hisses through the standing water at the gutter's edge. Two women pass under an umbrella, their laughter dissolving into the rain before it reaches me. Somewhere south of here, a siren winds down to silence like a song deciding not to finish.

No one looks at me.

No one ever looks at me.

That is both my gift and my grievance, depending on the night.

The light in her window goes out. Somewhere inside there,

my goldfinch moves through the ritual of leaving—the chore-ography of a woman who performs for a living and knows how to prepare a face for the dark. She will check her bag. She will check the lock. She will pull the door shut behind her with the careful click of someone who believes a deadbolt is the same thing as safety.

She is wrong about that.

My goldfinch will pass within half a block of where I am standing.

I will let her.

What she will not check is the latch on the fire escape window. She thinks it is locked, so she dismisses it. We are creatures of pattern. Patterns are a leash. I have spent considerable time understanding exactly where the leash ends.

I cross the street.

The building requires a code, which is an obstacle for men who have not been patient enough to learn the residents' habits. The couple in 3B leaves for the gym at ten-forty on weeknights and returns at twelve-fifteen. They hold the door for people they have seen often enough to feel they recognize them, which is to say, they hold it for me without looking at my face.

They never look at my face.

Such mistakes.

The elevator smells of takeout, fabric softener, and the chemical tang of a cleaning product. I ride it to four. The hallway is empty. The carpet is the shade of institutional beige that exists in many buildings where the landlord has concluded that tenants are temporary, carpets are permanent, and the math shakes out in favor of beige.

Her door is the third on the left.

I stand before it for a moment, breathing deeply. This

matters. It is part of the ritual that keeps the fence standing, acknowledging that a line exists even as I step over it.

The stain approves of ritual. It always has. It is, in the end, a thing possessing tremendous patience itself, and it recognizes that same quality in me as kindred things recognize each other, not with fanfare, but with the certain whir of something finding its frequency.

The lock takes eleven seconds.

I have timed it.

The apartment smells of teakwood, clean laundry, and the clove-and-smoky leather remnants of her perfume. The kitchen light is off. She is not home. She is at the club tonight. I know her schedule. Knowing is the closest thing I have to touching, for now.

My eyes lift. There's a stain on her ceiling too, smaller than mine, faint and brown at the edges near the molding. Different, but a stain all the same. Hers has no mouth, no patience, no long memory of damp and dark. Still, the sight of it feels like recognition.

My stain drifts in. *You're here*, it says. *Begin.*

I move through the apartment without turning on a light. I know it well enough. The chair pulled from the kitchen table. The books stacked on the floor beside the couch she keeps meaning to shelve. The water glass on the nightstand will be refilled before she sleeps.

I know her bedroom like I know my own.

I set the photograph on her pillow.

My scarlet tanager does not know yet that she has been chosen. She is sleeping right now in her own bed, just down the street, dreaming about nothing, completely unaware that her image is being left on the cotton of a stranger's pillow by hands that know what comes next.

Face down. Centered. Placed with a level of care that the

word *careful* does not begin to cover. Like, the word *"ocean"* does not adequately convey what happens to a man standing at the edge of one, feeling its scale fill his chest until there is no room left for anything as small as breathing.

I smooth the edge with my thumb.

This is the promise. This is what the detective who comes for my goldfinch after she is gone will find. I have written it for them with the same meticulous attention I bring to everything. When he kneels beside whatever remains of my goldfinch and turns this photograph over with his gloved hands, he will understand.

He will see her face.

He will realize she is next.

He will be too late.

Always too late.

I stand over her bed for a long time. The streetlamp bleeds through the secondhand curtains in long strips across the pillow.

Soon, the penny-taste says, patient and absolute.

Soon.

I leave the way I came.

The hallway is still empty. The elevator still smells of takeout and softener. The couple from 3B are not back yet. The building door closes behind me.

On the corner, I yank my hoodie over my head against the rain.

Four floors above me, her window is dark.

But not for long.

She will come home.

And when she does, she will find what I left on her pillow, and the composition will crossover into its final movement, and every last person who thought they understood the plot of this story will realize they have been sitting in the wrong seats.

Watching the wrong man.
Looking in the wrong direction entirely.
I shove my hands in my front pocket and walk into the rain.
Behind me, her building holds its breath.
And in front of me, somewhere inside my own, in the dark between the plaster and the sky, something that used to be a woman smiles.

Chapter Five

ROWAN

MUSIC THUMPS through The Midnight Hour with a decadent beat that settles at the base of my core.

The fire crawling over my skin has nothing to do with the bass, or the bills tucked into my garter, or the man I'm dancing for with his grabby hands and savage eyes that keep forgetting the rules.

Colored light smears across the fog, and through it all, someone's gaze pins me with enough force to feel. Hot. Almost tactile, dragging down my back like a fingertip tracing the notches of my spine, and my skin prickles in its wake the way it does before a storm breaks.

He doesn't watch me the same as the other men in here do. He doesn't have a slack mouth or a hungry lean. He's different. Still. Patient. An invisible hand guides the arch of my back, sketching the tingle between my legs before I consciously decide to feel it.

I find him through the strobes.

Same corner. Same shadow. Barely lit, completely frozen in place, while everyone else in the room poured around him like he was the one still point the dark had chosen for itself.

I let my body show my anger. He never approaches, and

I'm furious about that. I'd respect him more if he'd either come get his hands dirty or stop haunting my shifts.

Each sway of my hips is aimed at the far wall, *not* the man paying for this dance. The one watching is the one pulling strings beneath my skin. His stare sketches the outline of my curves, leading the tilt of my pelvis, claiming me from a distance he still hasn't had the balls to close. Not once in all the weeks he's been coming here.

The customer beneath me spreads his knees, and I sink onto his lap, grinding against the hard ridge of him through his jeans, my thighs bracketing his hips, palms braced on his shoulders for balance. The friction spikes a familiar thrill, honest in a way most things aren't. Proof of what I can do with nothing but my body and a rhythm.

But the man under me is far from the one I'm imagining.

It's the one in the corner, whose presence owns the room. Whose gaze feels like fingers slipping beneath the edge of my G-string and pressing where I'm wet and swollen.

The customer repositions, a needy hiss escaping through his teeth as he pushes up into the grind. Bourbon and cheap cologne flood my nostrils, and the sour musk of a man who started sweating the second I sat on him. He thinks this is for him.

No, honey.

Each circle of my hips is a conversation with the shadow at the far wall. My body responds as if it knows him.

Do I?

That little bird in the back of my throat stirs again, whispering I know you in a voice I still can't place. I force it down. Focus on the grind. Focus on the music. Focus on the fire coursing through me in thick, dizzying waves until my hips are moving with a mind of their own, deep and slow, meant only for him.

A groan barrels out of my customer's chest. Meaty fingers twitch on my thighs.

I slap them away without looking down. "No touching," I remind him, though it's not his fault I'm this wound up.

It's not him I'm riding. That's the problem.

I close my eyes and let myself have it. The stranger's hands are heavy, commanding, his voice a whisper at my ear. I picture him steering my pace, watching as I lose control with those dark, assessing eyes that never waver, never give me an inch of mercy.

The dick under me grows harder. The tension inside me pulls tight, then tighter, then snaps...unspooling in a sudden breathless rush that rolls through my legs, up into my chest, and breaks across my skin in a full-body tremor I couldn't hide if I wanted to.

When I open my eyes, the corner is empty. Nothing but wall and shadow. It's like he evaporated the second I broke.

A cold finger traces down my spine. "Where the hell did you go?"

My customer misreads everything, mistakes my shudder for gratitude, my stillness for invitation. His confidence swells on the wrong conclusion. His hands grow braver, sliding up my thighs, fingers nudging under the edge of my G-string, like he's earned something he hasn't paid for and couldn't buy anyway.

He thinks my body answered him. He has no idea I left him behind and used his cock as a convenient stand-in for someone who vanished into thin air.

"All right, gorgeous," his teeth graze my collarbone, "let's take this somewhere private."

"Not interested."

He laughs against my skin, hand flexing on my thigh. "You don't get that wet unless you want a man to finish it."

"I said *no*." I brace my palms against his chest and push.

He doesn't give me space. He yanks me into him, hands clutching, breath hot against my ear, grip climbing my thigh, testing how much I'll surrender before I scream.

"Don't play shy now." His voice is slick with certainty, and he bites down on my earlobe hard enough to sting.

I shove him backward and scramble off his lap. "Dance is over, asshole."

"Come on." He grabs at my waist, fingers hooking the band of my skirt. "You're playing fucking games."

A frayed wire in my chest snaps, starts throwing sparks. "Get your hands off me."

The man stands abruptly, his knee catching mine against the stage partition. Pain cracks through my kneecap and up into my hip. The lights flash red, then blue, painting his face in violent, lurching color. For one second, he looks exactly like what he is.

"You owe me." A thick finger jabs toward my face. "You got me all worked up, and now you're gonna—"

"Oh, I got you all worked up?" I bark out a laugh that tastes like salt and bile. "What a tragedy."

He reaches for me again. I reel back, and a voice booms through the noise like a wall coming down, "Hey."

Devon steps between us. Six-four, two-forty, and built like a door that doesn't open unless he says so. The customer's hand stops mid-reach.

"Hands off the dancers," Devon commands.

The customer scoffs. "She was asking for—"

"Don't." Devon puts one hand flat against the man's chest and moves him backward, the same as one would move furniture. "Don't argue. Don't finish that sentence. Out."

The guy staggers, eyes going wide, recalculating. "This is bullshit—"

Devon points at the exit. "Don't make me walk you."

The man's jaw works around something, swallows it, and storms toward the door, muttering curses that dissolve into the bass.

Devon turns to me. The granite drops out of his face. "You good?"

I nod. It's a lie, and he sees right through it.

My pulse skitters, but not because of the asshole who thought a lap dance was a down payment on access. My stranger watched as I dry humped that man. Watched me come all over his clothed dick. I used someone else's body to chase the phantom of *his* attention, then he disappeared the moment I shattered.

And what I don't get more than anything?

Is why his absence feels more violent than the man who put his hands on me.

Chapter Six

ELIAS

I WATCH her get off on another man's lap, and the part of me built for restraint cracks straight down the middle.

It's not anger coursing through me. Anger would be simple. Anger I could lock away and starve, like how I've starved many inconvenient feelings since the academy taught me how to stand over a body and take notes.

This is older. A territorial pulse starting in my jaw and sinking straight through my chest into the part I keep locked, the part that assesses and catalogs and *wants* with an awareness that scares the hell out of me if I look at it directly.

Sure, she rubbed her pussy on him until she cried out in ecstasy, but he didn't exist. Her eyes were locked on my corner the whole time, and each careen of her hips was aimed twenty feet past the man paying for the privilege, straight into the darkness where I stood with my arms crossed, pulse pounding in my teeth.

She came for *me*. Not him.

Then I left. Staying meant crossing the floor, putting my hands on her in a room full of witnesses, and I'm not a man who acts without a plan.

I've been watching her for weeks. I know the structure of

this place—the last song plays at 1:45, Devon Leclair—head of security—locks the side entrance at 2:10, the girls filter out the back in pairs between 2:15 and 2:30. I know which breaker box feeds the main floor because I traced the electrical panel two weeks ago during a walk-through I disguised as a noise-complaint follow-up. The panel is in the alley behind the kitchen, under a steel cover that doesn't lock because the latch broke in January, and the landlord never fixed it.

This city and its beautiful negligence.

I check my watch. It's 1:00 a.m. on the dot.

The alley reeks of dumpster runoff and of the kitchen grease trap that nobody emptied tonight. My fingers close around the main breaker—cold metal, heavy resistance—and I yank it down.

The bass dies first. The lights follow. The Midnight Hour goes dark in a single, sucking breath, as if the building itself closed its eyes.

The aftermath drifts out through shouts and curses.

Devon's voice booms over the noise, "Everyone off the floor. Now."

Emergency lights click on and pale blue rectangles light up over the exits, barely enough to see by. Through the kitchen door, I catch the shuffle of bodies moving toward the exits, the clink of glasses abandoned on tables, heels clicking fast on the concrete stairs.

The side door opens. The girls pour into the night in clusters, jackets thrown over costumes, phones lighting their faces. I count them from the shadows behind the dumpster.

A door slams open inside. Boots hit concrete. Devon appears, voice tight with irritation as he paces somewhere near the kitchen. I crouch further.

"Yeah, it's me," he snaps, phone to his ear. "No, not a surge.

Whole damn panel just dropped. I don't know—yeah, I checked the board, it's not coming back up." A pause. He exhales through his nose. "No, I'm not keeping people in here in the dark. You want lawsuits? Because that's how you get lawsuits."

Another pause. Longer this time.

"Fine. I'll shut it down, clear it out. Call the city, I'll lock it up." A second later, he's all business again. "We're done for tonight. Go home."

The bouncer scans the parking lot with the alert, methodical sweep of a man who takes his job personally. He doesn't glance toward the alley. No reason to. The breaker box is invisible from the lot, and he's not maintenance.

"Move it," Devon calls, not unkindly, just done. "We're closed." His gaze cuts across cars one more time, shadows, movement, everything—everywhere but where I am. "Ladies, if you left your shit inside, go grab it. Five minutes."

A ripple moves through the group. Groans, a few laughs, heels turning back toward the door. They file in again, less frantic this time, more annoyed than anything else.

I don't see her.

After a while, the flow thins. Voices fade as rides pull up and taillights bleed red across wet pavement. One by one, the girls disappear into the evening, the energy of the place draining out with them until the lot subsides into an emptier space.

Devon lingers in the doorway, jaw working, phone in his hand like he's debating another call. He drags a hand over his face and mutters something I can't catch.

I count the girls again.

In.

Out.

Faces lit by the wash of emergency lights and phone

screens, every movement is registered. Jackets, purses, keys clutched in hands.

Still counting.

Still waiting.

The last of them trickles out, zipping coats, adjusting straps, checking phones. Devon steps back into the doorway, blocking it with his frame, ticking through them with a glance that's all muscle memory.

"Everyone good?" he asks, halfway turned to lock up.

One of the dancers, purple hair, glitter clinging to her shoulders, pauses while digging through her purse for her keys.

"Hey," Devon says to her, frowning. "Where's Ro?"

Ro. Short for something longer, I presume.

Purple hair glances up. "She left already."

Devon freezes. "With who?"

She shifts her bag higher on her shoulder. "That guy."

"What guy?"

She gives him a look. "The one from her dance. The one she was all over."

His expression hardens. "What. Guy?"

Purple Hair sighs, impatient now. "The one she made a mess all over for a hundred bucks, Dev. Tall, dark, mean-looking, like he'd never smiled a day in his life. Him."

Devon's jaw locks. The phone goes still in his hand. "That's not like her."

"Yeah, well, she did." Purple Hair shrugs. "I saw her leave with him."

He looks past her toward the lot, thinking, recalculating, trying to decide whether this is a lie, stupid-Ro behavior, or danger.

"She say anything?"

"Nope. Just grabbed her stuff and went." Purple Hair digs

out her keys at last. "Honestly, I don't blame her. He had money, and probably a big dick."

Devon does not smile.

"You get a look at his car?"

"No." She squints up at him. "You good?"

"Fine." The word comes out flat and useless. He scrubs a hand over his mouth and continues staring into the lot. "Fine. Go home."

Purple Hair hesitates, then lifts one shoulder. "Night, Dev."

Devon waits until she's halfway to her car before pulling his phone back up and firing off a text, his thumb hitting harder than necessary. Probably to Ro.

After he's finished, "Jesus Christ, Ro," to no one at all, then turns, locks the door, and heads for his truck with the look of a man who's decided he'll swing by her place if she doesn't answer in the next ten minutes.

From the alley, I stare at the metal frame, rain ticking softly against the ground around me.

None of what that girl said is true.

Ro hasn't come out.

I would have seen her.

I see everything.

The thought burrows into place, silent and certain, sliding into the part of me that knew something was off the moment the count didn't add up.

I move before the echo of it fades. The kitchen door gives with a soft push. The smell hits first—grease, stale heat, a metallic tang under it. The emergency lights don't reach back here. Shadows pool in the corners, thick and undisturbed.

Slipping inside, I ease the door shut behind me, fingers finding the lock. A click. Sealed.

The noise out front mutes to nothing—only the thrum of a building settling into itself for the night.

I move through the kitchen without a sound, past stainless steel counters and stacked crates, toward the narrow hallway that feeds the main floor. The air there is cooler, calmer.

Taking a position near the side door, I wait. I'm good at waiting. Better than most people understand.

Devon locked the place from the outside.

Which means whoever's still in here...

is in here alone.

I check my watch again. 1:45.

The downlights throw a hazy golden wash through the front, enough to view the outline of the bar, the stage, the chairs left pulled away from tables where customers abandoned them mid-drink.

The place reminds me of a crime scene after the tape goes up, that eerie hush of a room that was full of life fifteen minutes ago and now holds only the residue.

My boots are quiet on the tile. A mixture of scents hangs in the upper reaches of the room, the sticky aftermath of spilled cocktails, the traces of a hundred bodies' worth of cologne, sweat, and perfume settling into the upholstery now that the ventilation is dead.

Underneath everything, threaded through the chemical fog like a vein of gold in dark rock, her scent—clove and smoky leather, and the headier note that lives close to her skin. It's lived within me since the night she sat down, and changed the architecture of my entire system.

Standing at the far edge of the main floor, near my corner —the place I've occupied for weeks now, learning the angles, memorizing the sightlines, filing all the entrances and exits and camera blind spots in a room I know better than the precinct bullpen by now, I wait.

The dressing room is behind the stage, down a short

hallway lit by a single emergency rectangle that makes the corridor look like the throat of something swallowed.

She's back there. I feel her. She's a match burning in a closed room. A displacement of silence. Warmth where there shouldn't be any.

Three minutes pass. I count them.

The dressing room curtain yanks open. She steps into the corridor holding her phone, its screen lighting her face in pale blue. She hasn't changed out of the tight black dress. Her bag is slung across her body, her hair is down, carrying a slight wave that the stage lights heat into it. From forty feet away, in the residual haze of a dead club, she is the most beautiful thing I've ever seen.

Truly devastating.

She's peering down at her screen, thumbs moving, texting Devon back, probably. Hopefully it's: *I'm fine, home safe.*

She rounds the corner of the stage, steps onto the main floor—

And stops.

Her whole body locks up. It's not out of fear, no, not yet, but the full-alert freeze of a woman whose instincts are better than she gives them credit for. Her chin comes up, hand moves to the strap of her bag, where I know, from the night I followed her home, keeping a manageable separation, so she never detected, the zipper sits six inches from the matte-black grip of a pistol she carries.

The emergency light is behind her, which means I'm a shadow in a room full of them. But she knows. Her body remembers.

"You can take your hand off the gun." My voice carries across the empty room, and I watch the words swirl in her brain—the micro-flinch in her shoulders, the intake of breath, how she leans onto her back foot as she calculates whether to run or draw.

Then her eyes adjust. Or maybe she recognizes my voice before the outline of me. I don't know which comes first. But I see the exact moment it hits her.

The tension in her spine doesn't relax. It *transforms*, goes from fear-taut to something I feel in the pit of my stomach like a fist unclenching.

Recognition crosses her face in waves. The stranger from the corner, his build, his posture, the set of his jaw in the dark.

Then deeper: the man from the bar, the one who counted her touches, the one who tasted her in the cab of his truck while the rain hammered the roof and the windows went white.

The detective who took her apart and held her afterward like she was something worth being careful with. The one who found her again because she's worth protecting.

All the same man.

All of them. Me.

I step out of the shadows and into the dim light, showing her who she's been dancing for from the stage.

"You?"

One word, voice barely above the buzz of the kitchen's backup generator, yet it carries across the room like a bird hitting glass.

"Oh, my god." Hand dropping from the bag strap, her phone screen goes dark in her grip. She stands in the middle of the empty club, ten feet from me. The pieces click into place behind her eyes—weeks of gazing out at me lurk in the corner, and fantasizing about me while grinding on another man's lap twenty minutes ago.

"Why?" Her throat moves. The swallow travels the full

length of her neck. She's not scared. This is rawer than scared. "You could've said something. You could've—"

"And what?"

She exhales a short, sharp breath that might be a laugh or might be an emotion she's not fully processing. "Showed me it was you."

I hold her gaze. The light carves her face into planes of indigo and shadow. She looks like the photograph I'm carrying in the evidence bag. It should be in lockup, not in my possession, and the fact that it isn't says more about me than I want her to know. "I should have. I didn't."

"Why?"

The honest answer is one I don't have language for. It lives in the section of me that counts minutes and measures the distance between wanting and having with an accuracy that would horrify her if she understood it.

What I say is, "Because you did something to me that night, and watching you was the only way I knew to stay sane. I was afraid that if I stepped into the light, whatever was holding me together would break."

She stares at me. "That is," she says slowly, "either the most romantic or the most fucked-up thing anyone has ever said to me."

The echo hits us both at the same time. She said it to me once before — *that's either the sexiest or the most terrifying thing anyone's ever said to me*—the night she changed the molecular structure of my life.

The corner of her mouth twitches. "So, you're my stranger." It's not a question.

"Yes."

She closes the space between us. Five feet. Three, moving exactly how she does on stage, the steps weighted with a gravity that sucks the air in the room toward her, but this is different. There's no performance in it. No pole, no beat, no crowd. Just her and me and the whisper of a dead building breathing around us.

She stops. Cloves and smoky leather invade my senses, gone warm from exertion. Mingled in is the faded bite of her hairspray, the salt of dried sweat at the hollow of her throat. Underneath that, something new, sharp, electric, adrenaline bleeding off her skin.

Her eyes are wet. She's not crying. But she's closer to it than I've ever seen her, and the sight of it twists my heart, pressurizes it, makes it *ache* in a way that has nothing to do with wanting her body and everything to do with wanting her all for myself. Only me.

No, mine, something whispers.

It's the word that lives in the dark room inside my brain that I don't enter. I push it down. Bury it.

She reaches up, fingers skating across my jaw cautiously, unsure of whether I'm real or not. Her touch is light, testing. The pads of her fingertips trace the line of bone from my ear to my chin. Her thumb finds the curve beneath my cheekbone, gentle and exploratory, sending a shudder through me so violent I have to lock my knees to stay standing.

"I left your truck a month ago, and some part of me is still in it with you."

"I know the feeling."

Her hand slides to the back of my neck and draws me to her.

The kiss isn't gentle. She's a woman who's been starving for a month and found the thing she's been hungry for. It's hot, open, her tongue in my mouth, fist in my shirt, and a sound in her throat that vibrates through my jaw, down into my chest. She tastes like mint, whatever drink she consumed earlier, and something underneath that's purely her—spicy, *mine*.

That word keeps surfacing. I bury it again.

My hands find her waist. I lift her, setting her on the edge of the bar. The wood is scarred beneath my palms, sticky with the residue of a hundred spilled drinks.

Her legs spread, and she pulls me between her thighs, the position putting her above me, looking down, her blonde hair falling around both our faces like a curtain shutting out the room.

The light catches her from behind, where the backup system bleeds through the bottle display. She looks like a painting done in bruises and fire.

"Hi." Breathless. Smiling. Her hand finds my face, thumb tracing the line beneath my eye.

"Hi."

"You cut the power, didn't you?"

"The breaker box is in the alley. Latch has been broken since January."

She laughs. That sound cracked my chest open the first night I heard it and has been living inside me rent-free ever since. "You *planned* this."

"I'm a detective." I shrug. "We plan things."

"You're a lunatic."

"Also possible."

Her legs tighten around me. The smile fades. A primal hunger replaces it, and her fingers slide from my cheek into my hair and grip. The grip sends a bolt of lightning straight down my spine and into the base of my cock.

"I came all over a customer's lap tonight," she admits, voice stable and absolutely lethal. "But I was looking at you the whole time."

"I know."

"That piss you off?"

"Yes."

"Good." She drags me closer by the hair. Her lips hover a breath from mine. "Now remind me why I was looking at you instead of him."

My hands slide under the hem of her dress, and the shock of her bare skin against my palms is smooth, goosebumped where the cold air has been sitting against her stomach. It's a revelation I would've never tired of. Shame.

I push the fabric up. She lifts her legs to let me, and for a second she's suspended there in the light, back arched, the lines of her body drawn in indigo and gold, and I have to stop. I have to look.

I have to memorize.

"You're staring."

"I'm always staring." My mouth moves to the center of her chest, between her breasts, and I breathe her in—cloves, the salt at her sternum, the zest of a lotion she put on hours ago that's now just *her*.

Lips tracing the line of her collarbone, my tongue finds the pulse at the base of her throat, and I hold my mouth there, counting the beats.

She shivers. "Why do you do that?"

"Do what?"

"Count." Her fingers tighten in my hair again. "You count my heartbeats."

I don't answer. She's right, and the reason she's right would undo everything if I let it surface.

My mouth travels down, kissing the swell of her breast above the edge of her bra, then I pull the fabric down, close my lips around her nipple, and suck, the flat of my tongue circling against her until her hips jerk forward.

She gasps, loud in the empty room, the sound bouncing off the mirrored walls and coming back to us doubled.

"*Fuck.*" Her head tips back. I feel the word vibrate through her ribcage against my mouth.

I take my time. The terrain of her body is similar to a crime scene. Each surface tells a story. Every reaction is evidence. I want the gasp when my teeth graze her nipple. The moan when my hand slides between her thighs and breaks through the thin layer of her G-string.

Her hips swivel into my palm like a question she already knows the answer to. "Off," she breathes, tugging at my shirt. "Take it off. I want to feel you."

I yank my hoodie over my head. Her hands are on my chest before it hits the floor, palms mapping the planes of me, nails dragging down my ribs, fingers tracing the scar below my left pectoral that she would've asked me about someday, and I would've lied about.

Her touch is greedy and reverent all at once. She leans forward, presses her open mouth to the base of my throat, tasting my skin. The sound I make is not civilized.

I hook my fingers into the barely existent string of underwear. "Lift."

She braces her palms on the bar and raises her hips.

I peel the scrap of black lace down her legs and toss it somewhere into the dark. The bar is cold beneath her bare thighs. She hisses at the contact, then laughs when my hands slip under her and yank her to the edge.

She's wet. Heat radiates off her, slick already on the inside of her thighs. When I slide two fingers through her, she bites her bottom lip so hard the color leaves it.

"God, you're—" I lose the end of the sentence. My mouth waters at the sight of her soaked, swollen, pussy gripping my fingers the second I push inside, and it's so tight, so hot, I have to press my forehead against her inner thigh and breathe through the noise in my head.

Mine. Mine. Mine.

My thumb circles her clit, stroking, curling, finding the spot I framed our first time, and pressing until her body starts shaking.

She grabs my shoulders, nails digging in. Her breathing fractures into small, sharp sounds that hit my ear like a language I'm the only person alive who speaks.

"I don't want your fingers," she manages. "I want *you.*"

Rising, I undo my belt. The sound of it—leather through loops, the metal clank of the buckle—echoes, and I watch her face when she hears it. Her pupils blow wide. Lips part. The sound obviously struck a memory from the truck.

The button gives. The zipper drags down tooth by tooth, and the relief of freeing myself from the denim is almost violent. I'm so hard it borders on pain. The tension has been building since she fucked that man's clothed dick with her eyes pinned on mine.

The cool air of the club hits me, and the contrast makes my cock twitch against my stomach, slick at the tip, aching with a need that's been building for weeks.

She glances down between us, and her breath catches. Thighs tightening around my waist, she hauls me closer, and the wet heat of her pushes against the length of me, hovering with a slick slide against my shaft.

"Condom," she breathes. Not a question. A rule.

I pull my wallet from my back pocket. The foil packet is warm from being compressed against my body all night. I tear it with my teeth—a sound that makes her bite her lip again—and roll it down my length with a hand that's steadier than it has any right to be, given that she's clocking each inch of the motion with those blue eyes blown black in the hazy light.

Her hand wraps around me over the latex, one slow stroke from base to tip, testing the thickness of me through the thin barrier. The groan that rips out of my chest could rattle the bottles behind the bar.

Her thumb drags across the head of my cock, and I stop breathing.

"That feel good?"

"Yes."

"Good. Now put that pretty cock to work."

Fuck this woman.

Lining myself up at her waiting entrance, I push into her in one unbroken stroke, and the world narrows to the place where we meet.

She's hot, tight, and hugging my cock before I'm fully seated. Her body pulls me deeper, as if it has its own gravity or hunger.

Her mouth falls open on a soundless gasp, hands flying to the edge of the bar and gripping until her knuckles go white. "Oh, God, you make me so full."

I don't move. Not yet. I hold myself inside her, looking at her, all flushed, trembling, backlit in bruising colors, and I deposit this moment inside the part of me that *hides*. The angle of her jaw. The shine of her eyes. How her chest rises and falls in shallow, shattered breaths.

Beautiful, the voice says. *Now she sees you.*

I bury it.

"Move," she demands. "Fuck me. *Please.*"

I draw back, then drive into her. The bar groans under us, the wood protesting, glasses rattling somewhere behind her, a bottle tipping over with a dull roll and clinking against another.

She cries out. "Fuck." The sound fills the empty club like a hymn in a cathedral.

Setting a deep, slow, punishing rhythm, each thrust pushes her back an inch on the bar top. I have to pull her back to me with my hands on her hips, the grip just shy of bruising, my thumbs pushing into the grooves above her hip bones, where I know from the truck she carries sensation like a wildfire.

"Right there," she gasps. "*Right fucking there.* Don't stop. I want you to make it hurt."

Angling my hips, I hit the spot that makes her walls cinch around me so hard I see stars, and I do it again, and again, building the tension is a tide that doesn't know how to recede.

Her legs lock around my waist. Her hand palms my cheek,

fingers curling into my jaw, tilting my head up so I'm gazing at her. She's flushed, shaking, eyes open and fixed on mine with an intensity that strips any mask I've ever built, leaving me bare and blinking in the light.

"I see you," she breathes. "I see you."

The words hit like a bullet I didn't know was coming.

Because she doesn't. She sees the detective. The man from the bar who counted her touches and her heartbeats. The stranger who watched her dance for weeks, who finally stepped into the light.

She doesn't see the rest.

And how she says it—with her hand on my face, body wrapped around mine, eyes wet and wide, completely trusting —makes me want to be the man she thinks she's looking at.

But he doesn't exist. Never will.

Burying my face in her neck, I bury myself to the hilt and piston into her, fucking my obsession like I can outrun what I am. Hard, deep, my breath ragged against her throat, her nails drag down my back, leaving marks I'll carry for days.

The bar shakes. The bottles rattle.

"Oh, God." The sound in her voice is the most sacred and the most damning thing I've ever heard.

She comes first. The build shows in the tremor of her thighs, the tightening of her walls, the catch in her breath that goes silent for one suspended second before it breaks, and when it breaks, it breaks *hard*.

Her entire body arcs off the bar top, pussy shaking and pulsing around me. With her fingers digging into my jaw, the sound she makes is raw, unperformed, nothing like the moan on the stage, *nothing* like the sound she gave the man in the chair.

This sound is *mine*. And mine alone. *I* created it.

Following her over the edge with my mouth against her

throat, teeth grazing her pulse, the orgasm rips through me with a violence that whites out my vision and leaves me braced against the bar with both hands while the room slowly, slowly reassembles itself around us.

For a long time, neither of us moves. Her arms are around my neck. My forehead rests against her. Her heartbeat is fast, slowing in increments, coming back to earth. I count the beats because I can't help it. That's what I do. Counting is the only form of prayer I've ever trusted.

The emergency lights hum. Somewhere behind the bar, the tipped bottle has rolled to the edge and is tapping gently against the rail.

"Have I finally earned yours?"

She laughs softly. "Rowan."

"Rowan," I repeat. "That's pretty."

Her fingers move through my hair, absent, like how one might pet an animal that's finally laid down to rest. "I probably shouldn't have given my name to a man who's been stalking me for a month and cut the power to my club to get another taste of me. I should be terrified of you."

The light catches the aftermath on her face—the flush, the shine, the damp at her temples. She's smiling. It's small, it's tired, and it's the most adorable expression I've seen on her since the circus story at the bar.

"Are you?"

Rowan traces the line of my jaw with one finger. Takes her time. "No. And that should scare me more than it does."

The words are still dangling between us when I kiss her. I don't decide to. My body decides for me, hand sliding to the back of her neck, mouth against hers, gentle, *so* gentle it surprises us both. She makes a small gasp against my lips, like she wasn't expecting tenderness from the man who fucked her on a bar in a building he blacked out.

Sometimes the softest touch carries the deadliest ruin.

I kiss her until her breathing steadies. Her hand rests against my chest, as if checking to see if my heart is still beating.

It is. For now, it beats only for her. That seems like enough.

We dress in the dark. It's slow, fumbling, punctuated by laughter when she can't find her underwear, mine when I adjust my shirt wrong.

She insists on fixing it herself, laughing again. It sounds different in a space this empty, bouncing and echoing, and for a moment, the room feels almost safe. Almost normal.

I reset the breaker on our way out. The building shudders back to life behind us—lights, music, ventilation—and by the time we hit the sidewalk, rain has formed into a fine, drifting mist that hangs in the streetlight glow, suspended between falling and floating.

Rowan takes my arm without asking. Her hand slips through the crook of my elbow, fingers curling into the fabric of my hoodie, and the intimacy of the gesture is so small, so ordinary, it does more damage than anything that happened back at the club.

We walk four blocks. Her count, from the conversation with Devon she doesn't know I overheard. The streets are empty, slick with rain. The only sounds are our footsteps, the distant wail of a siren winding down somewhere south of us, and the occasional hiss of a car passing on the cross street.

She talks. I let her. She asks how I found the club. I tell her the truth—the noise complaint, the accident of walking in and seeing her on the stage.

"This is me," she says, gesturing to a tall building. It's new, glass and steel, the lobby lit in that cold corporate hue that passes for modern. She digs for her keys. Her fingers aren't shaking anymore, like they were in the club.

Mine are, though.

"Come up." The request is simple. A woman holding a door open for a man she's decided to trust.

I should say no. I should leave and come back tomorrow with a badge, a partner, and the professional mask this situation demands.

Instead, I follow her inside.

The elevator is bright after the dark street, and in the overhead light, I see what I did to her. A flush stains her chest, there's redness at her throat, where my stubble scraped, and a faint bruise already forming on her hip where the edge of the bar dug in, along with my grip.

Rowan catches me looking and doesn't cover up. She leans against the elevator wall, watching me watch her. There's a veneration in the look she's giving me that makes the locked thing in my chest twist painfully.

Her apartment is cute. Lived-in. Smells like a teakwood candle she burned earlier in the week. She drops her bag by the door, kicks off her heels, and pads barefoot into the kitchen for a glass of water.

I stand in the entryway and breathe.

Something is wrong.

It's faint—almost nothing—but the air carries a note underneath the candle that doesn't belong. Rot. Mineral. The cold-stone scent of a place where light doesn't reach.

That should stop me. Should send me out the door, down the elevator, back into the rain where I can think clearly, where that scent loses its hold on the air around me.

But I stay. Let her hand me a glass of water, let her lean against the kitchen counter, and look at me with those blue eyes that have no idea what's burning a hole in my pocket.

"You got quiet," she notes.

"I've got something I need to tell you."

The veneration that was in her face morphs. It's not gone —merely rearranged, like how a room does so when someone opens a window, and the draft moves through it.

"That sounds like a cop voice."

"It is."

She crosses her arms. The strap of her dress slips off her shoulder—the same shoulder, always the same one, just like at the bar—and she doesn't fix it.

"Okay, detective." The pulse jumping at the base of her throat gives her fear away. I count it without meaning to. "Tell me."

I gaze at her. This woman who danced for me in the dark. Who came apart in my arms less than an hour ago. Who gave me her name after I made her come all over my cock, like it was nothing, like it wasn't the most dangerous gift she could've offered.

I'm about to tell her about the dead woman with green eyes and the photograph left at the scene. That someone is watching her. That they got close enough to photograph her while she slept. That she is not safe.

I'm going to tell her all of this with my fingerprints still drying on the glass in her kitchen, and she's going to trust every word.

"There was a murder two nights ago," I say. "A woman in her apartment on the east side. Strangled."

Rowan's arms tighten across her chest.

"We found a photograph at the scene that wasn't of the victim." I hold her gaze. "It was of you."

The color leaves her face in a single, silent wave, like a tide pulling back from sand.

"Rowan." My hand finds her elbow, thumb settling into the crook of it, against the warm skin there. Her pulse hammers through the thin barrier of vein and tendon. "I'll keep you safe."

The words leave my mouth, and I hear them the way she hears them—protective, urgent, the voice of a man who cares.

I hear them another way, too. How the dark hears them. And *she* smiles.

Keep her.

Rowan doesn't speak. When she looks up at me with those wide, blue eyes full of agonizing fear and asks me to stay, I say yes.

I will always say yes.

Chapter Seven

ROWAN

THE WORDS DON'T LAND ALL AT once.

They arrive in pieces, like how a window breaks: first the crack, thin and almost silent, then the whole thing coming apart in a rush that leaves you standing in a pile of shards with no memory of how you got there.

Photograph.

Crime scene.

Me.

My arms are crossed so tight my fingernails are digging crescents into my own biceps. The cold tile of the kitchen floor seeps through my bare feet, the hum of the refrigerator behind me, the drip of the faucet I keep meaning to fix. All the small, domestic sounds amplify to a scream by the silence between his words and mine.

Elias is watching me. He's always watching. I know that now. My body knew it weeks before my brain caught up.

But what he's doing right now is different. His hand is still on my elbow. There's an emotion behind his eyes that looks less like a man comforting a woman and more like a man bracing for an impact he knows is coming.

"Say that again," I manage.

"A woman was murdered in her apartment two nights ago." His voice is level. Cop voice. The one that categorizes the world into facts and holds the feeling at arm's length. "We found a photograph at the scene. Of you."

"Me?"

"You."

The kitchen shrinks. Even the teakwood in the air goes wrong, turning resinous and stale, like damp wood trapped behind a wall. My stomach turns.

His thumb strokes the crook of my elbow. "I recognized you immediately." Something crosses his face, fast, like a shadow passing over a window. "There's no question."

I pull my arm out of his grip. It's not that I don't want him touching me—I do, I want him to hold me together because the seams are starting to pull—but I need to move, or I'm going to come apart standing still.

"It was of you sleeping," he explains further. "Which means they've been inside your home."

I walk three steps and stop. Then two more. My kitchen is too small for pacing, but I'm pacing anyway, feet roaming over tile, arms wrapped around myself like I'm trying to hold my ribcage in place.

"Sleeping?" I repeat. "Someone photographed me *sleeping?*"

Elias's pause is louder than any word he could give.

I turn to look at him, standing in the exact spot I left him, hands at his sides, and his face has gone into careful and controlled mode, the expression of a man who's managing what he shows.

"Yes," he finally answers. "The perp we're looking for is careful. Methodical. Probably mid-thirties. Keeps trophies. Photographs, most likely. They've been doing this a long time without anyone noticing. Probably does shift work. Might be starting to escalate. I don't want you going to work alone until we have him."

The sound that comes out of me isn't a laugh. More of a failed attempt at one. The exhale I make is the result of the universe dealing me something so grotesque my body doesn't know whether to scream or fold.

"Are you serious?"

His brows knit together.

"You're kidding, right? This is a joke? This is payback for me telling you I grew up in the circus. That's what this is about?"

Elias reaches into his hoodie and pulls out a clear plastic bag. Through the plastic, a photograph stares back at me—a woman, blonde, asleep. The sheet is twisted around her hips. One bare shoulder catches a streetlamp's glow through half-open curtains. Her mouth is slightly parted. Her hand rests near her throat, fingers curled.

Pretty. A shot someone might take of a lover in the early morning, tender and intimate, until—

I don't react at first. The brain protects you like that, gives you a half-second of ignorance, a thin membrane of *that can't be what I think it is* before the truth punches through.

But that's my ring. The silver one on my index finger, the one my sister gave me, the one I never take off. It catches the streetlight in the photograph, the same way it's catching the kitchen light right now, as my hand grips the counter so hard my tendons stand out like cables.

And that's my pillow. My headboard. The curtains I bought at a secondhand shop on Ninth, because I liked how the light came through them in the morning. The water glass on my nightstand that I refill each night before I turn off the lamp.

That's *me*.

The revelation arrives everywhere at once, except in my brain. My skin goes cold. Stomach flips. Every hair on my arms lifts, and the back of my neck prickles with the phantom sensation of being watched, being *studied*, by someone who was close enough to touch me. Close enough to hear me breathe.

I was asleep when it happened, probably dreaming about nothing, while an intruder stood over me, holding a camera with the diligence of a man—or woman—who had all the time in the world.

The floor drops out. My legs stop working, and I'm grabbing for the counter, knuckles cracking against the granite edge. A sound comes out of my mouth that's less than a word and more than a breath, animal, involuntary, the noise a body makes when it recognizes danger.

"That's me," I whisper. As if he doesn't know. As if saying it out loud will make it less true, rather than more. I sound more out of sorts when I add, "Elias, that's my *bedroom*."

His hands hold me upright. "I know, Rowan."

My voice sounds like it's coming from the bottom of a well. "They stood over my bed and took a photograph, and I didn't —I never—"

Shoving the heels of my hands into my eyes until sparks ignite, I breathe through my teeth. The air in my apartment tastes wrong. Moldy. Evil. I smelled it earlier today, after I got home from the gym. I couldn't place it, but it made me lock the deadbolt, slide the chain, and reach for my gun.

Elias peels my hands away from my face. His expression hasn't changed, but something beneath it does—a tectonic shift, invisible on the surface, but felt in the room like a pressure change before a storm. He looks at me for a long time. "Show me."

"Show you what?"

"Your apartment. Each room. I need to check if anything's been moved, tampered with, or taken."

The cop voice is fully online now. He's not the man who

kissed me gently on a bar top over an hour ago—he's the detective, scanning my kitchen with eyes that are filing away every surface, object, and angle with the same precision he used to count my heartbeats.

The transformation is seamless and absolute. He crossed a line inside himself, and now he's on the other side of it. I don't know whether that should make me feel safe or terrified, given how quickly he made the switch.

"Living room," I say, gesturing to it.

Elias moves through my space, touching nothing but seeing everything. He checks the windows. The locks. Runs his gaze along the baseboards, the door frame, the hinges. His fingers hover near the latch of the fire escape window, and I observe that same shadowy flicker across his face. Fast. Gone before I can second-guess whether I even saw it all.

"This lock's been tampered with. See the scratches on the plate? Someone forced it and closed it behind them."

My stomach drops through the floor.

"Bathroom." He moves on. Intense and thorough.

The bathroom is clear. The shower curtain is pulled back. I always leave it like that. Nothing touched. Nothing wrong. But the air is thinner, or maybe that's my lungs refusing to fill properly.

We stand in the hallway outside my bedroom door. I don't want to go in. The feeling hits me with the force of a full-body refusal, all my nerves firing *no*, in a chorus that starts in my feet and climbs to the base of my skull.

My bedroom is the safest room in my world. It's where I lay my head, and I breathe in my own quiet space. It's where I sleep with the lamp on sometimes because the dark still scares me, if I'm being honest. It's the room I lock the rest of the world out of.

And someone was in it. Standing over my bed. Watching me.

"Rowan." Elias's voice has changed again. Soft now. Not the cop. The man. His hand finds the small of my back. "You don't have to go in first. I can—"

"No." I push the door open. "It's my room."

The bedroom is dark. The streetlamp outside bleeds through the curtains in a wash of sodium yellow, painting everything in shades of coral and shadow. The bed is made—I always make my bed, a compulsion I inherited from a mother who believed in the religion of hospital corners and smooth surfaces. My nightstand holds a glass of water from this morning, a hair tie, the book I'm halfway through, and a receipt marking my page.

Everything is where I left it.

Except...

There's a photograph on my pillow.

Face down. Centered precisely on the white cotton. Positioned with a care that makes my skin crawl. It's *placed* as one might place a love letter. Or lay flowers on a grave.

"Don't touch it." Elias barks behind me. His firm hand is on my shoulder now, drawing me back from the bed. "Rowan. Don't touch it."

"I wasn't going to." My hands are shaking too badly to touch anything. I'm staring at the white rectangle on the white pillow—and the wrongness of it is so total, so complete, that the room feels like it's tilting on an axis.

Elias moves past me, pulls his sleeve over his hand, and uses the cuff to carefully flip the photograph over.

It's upside down from where I'm standing, but I don't need to see it right side up to know what it is.

A woman. Red hair fanned across a pink silk pillow. Asleep. One hand rests on her stomach, fingers slightly curled. Like mine were. Her lips are parted on a breath she doesn't know is being captured. A gold watch curves around her wrist, catching the light from a window just out of frame.

She's beautiful. She's peaceful. She has no idea someone is standing over her bed.

The image hits me like a mirror held at the wrong angle. It's not my face or my hair. It's not my room, but it's *my* photograph. The same violation. The same stolen intimacy. The same patient, suffocating closeness of a lens held by some psycho who stood in the dark and decided this woman's privacy was worth taking.

"I don't know her." My voice comes out strange. Thin. Like it's been stretched over something jagged. "Elias, I don't—who is she?"

He's leaning over the photograph without touching, studying it the same way I've seen him study me, assessing, filing, counting details with an accuracy that would be clinical if not for the rigid set of his jaw and the tendon jumping in his neck.

"I don't know," he says, straightening. "Not yet."

"It's the same—" I can hear the fracture in my own voice. "It's the same as mine. So, this is what he does then? He kills women and leaves photos of the next victim..." My words trail off.

Elias approaches.

"I'm next, aren't I—" I can't finish the sentence. My mouth shapes the words, but my throat locks around them like a fist closing.

Somewhere in this city, the woman in the photo is breathing against her pillow with her gold watch resting on the pulse of her wrist, and she doesn't know. She doesn't know that a killer has stood in her room and memorized the geography of her sleeping body. Doesn't know that her photograph is lying on a stranger's pillow.

She doesn't know she has an expiration date.

And neither did I.

"He's telling me," I croak. The understanding rises slow and freezing, filling me from the feet up. "I'm just one stop in a line of victims who never saw him coming. He can reach into anyone's life. Somewhere, right now, another woman is asleep inside his plans."

Elias straightens. His face is a mask I can't read—something locked behind it, pressurized, held in place by a control that looks like it costs him everything. "He's telling us he's not finished."

I look at the woman in the photograph. I want to reach through the image and shake her awake. I want to scream at her—*lock your windows, check your doors, look behind you, look UP, there is someone in your room, and by the time you realize it, it will be too late.*

But she can't hear me. She's frozen in a moment she'll never know was stolen, the same way I was frozen in mine—asleep, trusting, dreaming about nothing while a monster stood close enough to touch and chose, for one more night, not to.

"We have to find her." I look at Elias.

That shadow crosses his face again. There and gone, so fast I almost miss it, like a door opening onto something vast and dark before it slams shut again.

"I will," he says, so certain and absolute, it makes me believe him completely.

I nod, then drift toward my bathroom.

"Rowan." Elias is in front of me. Both hands on my face. His palms are warm, dry, and steady, and I focus on the texture of his skin, the calluses at the tips of his fingers, the specific force of his thumbs against my cheekbones, because everything else in the room has gone liquid and unreliable. "Look at me." His voice is the only solid thing left. "Breathe. Look at me and breathe."

His eyes are dark. Darker than I've ever seen them. The muscle in his jaw jumps, his nostrils flare, and there's a tension running through his body that vibrates through his hands into my face, barely contained, barely controlled, a man holding a door shut against some enormous force.

"He's going to kill me," I whisper.

Elias shakes his head. "I'll protect you. Keep you safe." His thumbs stroke my cheekbones. "He's not here. I am. And I'm not leaving."

I want to believe him. I want to fall into the assurance of his voice the way I fell into his body earlier—fully, recklessly, without asking the questions I should be asking.

But a woman's face was on the place where I lay my head. And the man standing in my bedroom is a homicide detective who found a matching photograph of *me* at a murder scene. The distance between those two facts is a bridge swaying beneath my feet.

"Are there more?" My voice doesn't sound like mine. "Others?"

"I don't know yet. This is the first case we've come across with this signature."

"But you think it's the same person. The one who took the photo of the other woman. Of me. The one who killed—"

"Yes. It's the same person."

"What was the victim's name?"

He hesitates. "Miriam Walker."

"What are you going to do with the photo?"

"It's evidence." He says it gently, but the wall behind the

words is steel. "I'm going to call it in. Get a team here. And then I'll take you somewhere safe."

"I'm not leaving my apartment."

"Rowan —"

"I'm *not leaving*." It comes out sharper than I meant it to, and I hate the tremor underneath. "This is my home. Nobody gets to take that from me. It's the only thing I have. And whoever it is, doesn't get to stand over my bed and leave a sick little calling card just to make me *run*."

Elias watches me. I see the calculation happening—the detective weighing protocol against the woman in front of him, who's about to shatter if he pushes too hard.

He exhales through his nose. "Okay. I'll call my partner, but I'm staying with you tonight, and tomorrow we're having a real conversation about your safety. Non-negotiable."

"Fine."

"Go take a hot shower. Relax."

I nod.

"And you don't go near that bed until CSU has processed the room. I'm waiting on confirmation from them."

I look at my bed. *My* bed, with its white sheets, hospital corners, and pillows that smell like my shampoo and now hold the face of a woman who's in danger like me, and I'll never be able to unsee her.

"I wasn't planning on it," I say quietly.

Elias pulls out his phone. While he makes the call—voice spouting out clipped sentences, the shorthand of a man who's reported scenes like this a hundred times, I grab my own phone and move into my bathroom, wrap my arms around myself, and try to stop shaking.

I can't.

The rot and mold scent from earlier is back, and it's stronger in here, layered into the air like a stain I can't scrub out. Whoever was here spent time. Long enough to leave the photograph and long enough to *be* in this room. To stand where I'm standing. Breathe what I'm breathing. Learn me.

The thought sends ice water through my veins. With my back against the wall, I slide down until I'm sitting on the floor, knees pulled to my chest. The plaster is cold through my dress. The light is bright. Everything is heightened, too present. The dim haze of the club, the bar top, Elias's mouth on my throat now feels like it happened to a different woman in a different life.

In the other room, Elias is talking, his voice terse yet calm. Detective voice. Meant to stabilize a scene. Or to make a person feel safe.

Waiting for a moment when he isn't looking directly at me, I lift my phone, shielding the screen against my bent knee so the light doesn't spill across the bathroom. My fingers are trembling so hard that I miss the keyboard twice before I get it right.

> Love you.

> Just needed to say it.

I hit send to Devon, lock the screen, and slip the phone back into my pocket just as Elias's footsteps come closer.

He crouches in front of me, doesn't tell me it's going to be okay, avoids feeding me platitudes or rubbing my back, or saying any of the useless, meaningless things people say when the world has tilted off its axis.

Elias sits down next to me on the floor. Shoulder to shoulder. His body is hot against my side. He smells like the cold outside, the bar, and sex. There's something underneath that I can't place.

I lean into him. He lets me.

"I'm scared." It costs me something to admit it. More than I want.

Elias's arm comes around my shoulders. He pulls me into him, and I allow myself to be pulled. His chin rests on the top of my head. His heartbeat thumps through his chest—steady, steady, steady.

"I know. I've got you."

Pressing my face into the fabric of his hoodie, I inhale, breathing him in, and try to believe that the man holding me on the floor of my bathroom is exactly what he seems—a man who held me, a detective who found me, came back for me, and will stand between me and the monster hunting me in the dark.

That little bird in my throat has gone eerily quiet.

For the first time, its silence scares me more than its song.

Chapter Eight

YEARS on the job take me from a mental haze to alert in the space of a single blink when the sound of footsteps on hardwood causes me to bolt upright.

The apartment is dark except for the spill of light leaking from the kitchen—the under-cabinet LEDs she left on when we stopped talking and started surveying the apartment. An amber glow casts across the counter, and the two water glasses are still sitting where we left them.

The rest of the room holds its breath in shades of indigo and charcoal. Rain taps against the windows in a slow, irregular Morse code. The refrigerator hums. The baseboard heater clicks, then sits. Her place at three in the morning sounds like a living thing trying to sleep.

Rowan steps into the edge of that amber spill, and everything in me locks into place—spine, jaw, hands, the air in my lungs.

Her hair is darker when wet, falling in loose tangles past her shoulders. Droplets sit on her collarbone, one traces a slow path down the center of her chest, disappearing into the neckline of a cropped tee so thin that the shadow of her body shines through it. She's not wearing a bra. Her nipples are tight beneath the fabric—from the cold, from the hour, from something else entirely. My gaze, hopefully.

Black sleep shorts sit low on her hips, barely there, existing as a suggestion rather than a garment. Bare legs. Bare feet. Skin is tinged pink from the shower, on her knees and the insides of her elbows.

The scent of her lotion carries across the room: blackberries, a hint of vanilla mixed with mint shampoo, and the clean bite of whatever soap she used. Underneath all of it, the smell of her skin when it's been scrubbed clean cuts through the stale air of the apartment like a blade through cloth.

Blue eyes find mine across the dim room, and the look in them is not the look of a woman who's learned she's living inside a nightmare, though the last twenty-four hours have earned her every type in the catalog. No—this is something else. Awake and aimed.

Her body mistakes danger for desire, or perhaps it understands before the mind does that the two have always shared a border. Rowan's fear doesn't make her retreat. Instead, she burns brighter, every nerve turned outward, all instincts reaching for sensation, desperate enough to drown out the dark.

I should hate that I know this about her. My knowledge could be mistaken for manipulation. But I see the way terror makes her restless and hungry and achingly alive. And I understand it because some ruined part of me is built the same way.

My cock responds as she crosses the room in leisurely steps. Her shadow stretches and compresses on the hardwood as she passes through the kitchen light, back into the dark, and then into the faint white glow near the couch.

She stops in front of me. Her knees brush mine. The

residual heat of the shower radiates off her shins—or maybe that's my own temperature, climbing fast, blood thickening in my veins.

The air between us smells like her shampoo and the rain outside and the faint, lingering coffee I made while she was in the shower, when I decided neither of us could pretend we were going to sleep tonight. I spotted the bag of grounds in her cabinet the same way I spotted the books on her floor, the locks on her windows, and the scratch marks on the fire-escape latch. My process is automatic, compulsive, exactly how I process the rooms I choose to enter.

Counting.

Filing.

Keeping.

"Feel better?" My voice comes out low and rough.

Rowan shakes her head. A drop of water falls from a strand of her hair and lands on my knee, soaking through the denim in a small circle. She watches it happen. Doesn't apologize. Doesn't move.

"I need—" Her eyes drop to my mouth, stay there, fixed, studying with an intensity that makes the tendons in my neck pull taut. "—something."

I scoot forward. The couch cushion sinks beneath me, the leather creaks, and in the silence of her apartment, the sound is obscenely loud.

"Rowan..." Her name leaves my mouth like an exhale I've been holding for a month, and the sound of it hangs in the air, and I can't take it back.

I should stop this. Slow it. Do the decent thing, the *professional* thing, the thing the badge in my jacket pocket and the case file in my head require of me.

I should listen to that voice. Except, I didn't at the bar

when she looked at me with that reckless, honey-dark fire, and I fucked her against polished wood as if I'd never worn that badge a day in my life. I didn't listen when I followed her into the rain. Or when I walked into her apartment and stayed.

That voice has been losing to Rowan for a month now.

And she's scared. Vulnerable. A woman who found out hours ago that a killer has been in her bedroom, and the man sitting on her couch is the detective assigned to her case.

"The team will be here in an hour or so to process the scene."

Rowan slides her fingers into my hair. The touch is subdued, fingertips against my scalp, threading through the strands above my ear with a gentleness that doesn't match the look in her eyes. The contrast of soft hands and hard want sends heat sprinting through my center, then detonates south of my belt.

"Plenty of time, then." Rowan's running on adrenaline, fear, the recklessness of a woman who's stared down her own mortality and decided the answer is to *feel* something, *anything*, that isn't terror.

She isn't trembling. Isn't crying. She's not the fragile, broken thing the situation is trying to turn her into. This woman is lit from the inside, eyes wide, chest rising fast beneath that paper-thin shirt, the lines of her body angled toward me like a compass needle finding north.

"What do you need?" My voice fractures on the last syllable.

Her thumb traces the line of my jaw, following the bone from my ear to my chin. She did this in the club, the same path, pressure, same devastating patience.

"You came for me." Rowan's thumb rests beneath my bottom lip. "You stayed." Her breath stirs the air, mint, spice. I taste it on my next inhale. "I feel safe with you."

Safe.

The word sinks into me like a stone into dark water, falling through each layer of what I am—the detective, the man on the couch, the monster underneath that I don't let breathe—and settles at the bottom, in the silt, where I keep the truths that would end me if I spoke them out loud.

She feels safe.

My hands lift on their own, palms finding the backs of her thighs. They're impossibly smooth, the skin still damp at the crease behind her knees where the towel didn't quite reach. I draw her forward half an inch. The insides of my wrists feel the warmth of her through the fabric of her shorts.

Rowan's hips rock toward me, her body answering mine in a vocabulary that bypasses every conscious decision either of us could make. The tee rides up as she moves, exposing a stripe of bare stomach, the shallow dip of her navel, the soft line of muscle that runs down each side of her abdomen.

My hands continue to roam, gliding up over the curve of her ass, palms spreading wide, giving her the seconds she needs to stop me. The thin layer of her shorts is nothing but a whisper between my skin and hers.

Rowan's muscles tense and release under my grip as she processes the feel of my hands on her body. Her fingers tighten in my hair, guiding my head back, tilting my face up toward hers. The pull is gentle and absolute. I go where she tells me because I've been hers since she sat down beside me and told me she was raised by circus performers.

I breathe her in again. Mint, clean skin, and an animalistic scent underneath that no soap can wash away. It lives at the base of her throat and in the creases of her body. I've been tracking it ever since our first time together.

"I need you to make me forget about all this," she confesses, voice dropping into more of a vibration than a word.

It's a secret she's handing me with both hands. "For a little while, at least."

My fingers hook into the waistband of her shorts. The elastic stretches. The fabric pulls. She nods. The permission hits dead center in my chest like a key turning in a lock.

I ease the shorts down her hips. Slowly. *So* slowly I'm able to track each emotion that crosses her face—the slight catch of her breath, how her stomach contracts, the flutter of her lashes when they clear her hipbones.

As the cool air touches her skin, she watches me with such trust, and the version of herself she doesn't show on stage. No bills folded behind this. No performance. Or transaction.

This is human. And it's hers.

The shorts pool at her ankles. She steps out of them, one foot, then the other. The act is small. The sound of the fabric hitting the hardwood is hardly a whisper, but it's the loudest thing in the room.

Rowan stands before me in a T-shirt and nothing else. The truth of that—the bare skin, exposed vulnerability, absolute absence of armor—dries my mouth to dust.

Hunger gathers behind my teeth, taut as a wire. Something old and patient flickers awake in the deep water of my blood. It opens its eyes. Sees her. For a suspended, airless second, I forget how to be anything but *want* and *need*.

In an unconscious movement, my tongue drags across my lower lip—the motion of a man tasting something that isn't there yet but will be.

I look up at her. She looks down at me. The silence hums through the cushions, into the floor, and up through the soles of her bare feet. Her pulse is jumping, at her throat, at her wrist, in the subtle rise and fall of the vein that runs along the inside of her thigh.

I count it.

I always count.

Rowan places one knee on the couch beside my hip. The leather protests. Then the other knee, on the other side, and she's climbing into my lap with the measured grace of a woman who's about to take exactly what she wants.

While her hands clutch my shoulders, my palms coast up her legs to her hips, thumbs finding the notch above her hipbones, securing her there while her body perches over mine. She presses down, just right against me through the denim, making my vision blur at the edges.

Her breath catches. Mine stops.

Rowan leans in, forehead pressing against mine. The tips of our noses touch. Her eyelashes kiss my cheekbone when she blinks, and her mouth hovers a breath from mine. The air we're sharing is sweet and charged with an emotion that has no name and doesn't need one.

"Elias?"

"Yes."

"Make me yours. Keep me here. Don't let me leave this moment."

Make me yours.

My grip tightens on her hips. Her bones shift beneath my palms. Her pulse pounds through her skin, faster than before, a hummingbird rhythm that matches the one hammering against the inside of my own ribs.

Keep me. The words hit the part of me I lock up tight, fitting there perfectly, like they were always meant to live in that dark, silent room, and the thing behind the door stirs in its sleep and smiles.

My mouth lifts. The first contact is small, the brush of my bottom lip against hers, dry, electric, a question asked with skin instead of sound.

Rowan exhales into it. A shudder runs through her body

and into mine through each point of contact—her knees against my hips, her hands on my shoulders, her forehead against mine.

Then she opens her mouth.

And the world falls away.

Chapter Nine

BEFORE I CAN BLINK, his mouth is on mine, fast and savage, tongue sweeping past my lips in one consuming glide.

Cedar. Salt. Wet stone.

The scent of him floods my nose. It's a memory I've been keeping tucked between my ribs since the last time.

Something rises out of me and pours straight into him. My body answers a call it was born knowing. *Desire.*

I can taste the intent underneath. Consumption. Recognition. A thread of copper, light, like he's bitten the inside of his own mouth trying to be careful with me.

A strong arm cinches around my waist and drags me flush against him until I can't tell where I end, and he begins.

There's no asking. No easing. My hands fist in his shirt with a desperation I didn't know I had in me, and the rush that rips through me isn't heat. It's that thing I've been pretending isn't real—a pull so fierce it feels alive, as though it's been breathing in the room with us the whole time.

I'm falling, but Elias catches me like how a storm catches a door—force, not choice.

His mouth crashes back into mine. A sound detonates inside my chest, mine or his, I can't tell. He twists us, prone on the couch, his body pressing through the cotton of my shirt like I'm not wearing one at all. The cry that rips out of me gets swallowed before it forms.

I've felt men. Dozens. Scraps of them. Years of taking whatever crumbs they offered across the rim of a stage. But this man is tender. Relentless. The restrained violence in his grip says he heard the word I didn't speak.

He took his sweatshirt off and draped it over the arm of the couch. He's wearing a black T-shirt. My hands tug at it, needing skin, needing the current to deepen. He doesn't appease me. Doesn't slow. He handles me like I'm not fragile, as if he knows my sickness and isn't afraid to meet me inside it.

A thrill rips through me at the mystery of that, at the dangerous draw that owns me now. I'm chained to it.

He leans back so his lips have access to roam the line of my neck, and every part of me rises up to him. His breath skims my pulse. Stops there. Stays. Long enough that I feel him take it in—the jumping rhythm under my jaw—he's counting the number of it.

He's just tasting me, I tell myself.

My skin prickles.

The sharp edge under his attention feels dulled only because I'm running on fear and a day and a half without sleep. He senses it. He notices everything. I'm holding back by sheer survival instinct, and the thought of what I'll be like when I'm not a cracked vessel. He'll finally see me whole. That possibility makes a shiver ripple down my spine.

Elias moves against me, hips pushing into mine. The sound that slips out is involuntary, heartbreakingly honest. He captures it with another kiss, and the echo shimmers in my stomach.

There are too many layers muffling the contact my nerves

are begging for. Before I can fix it, his hands find the hem of my shirt. He yanks fast. The cotton rips easily, like paper tearing.

A gasp leaves me. Cool air hits my skin. So does his gaze. He's seen me before. But this feels different, like fingertips trailing over me in the dark, or a held breath—something closer to worship and devotion, and that from him feels heavier than any palm I've ever had on my body.

His hand curves around my breast. Firm. The pressure borders on bruising. I'm bowing toward it, craving it, begging him to meet the inferno burning inside me instead of flinching from it.

I've been handled like property. Too many hands that only wanted the outside. He doesn't touch me like that. He touches me as if each inch matters, and no part of me can be overlooked.

"You're so fucking perfect, Rowan." A guttural growl escapes him, and the air turns metallic, the same it does the second before lightning strikes, bright, thin, electric at the back of my tongue.

My nails dig into the shirt he still hasn't discarded. He watches me with that thirst that makes my heartbeats ricochet, and I realize he's counting them under his thumb where it rests at my collarbone.

Attentive, I tell myself. *He's just attentive.*

My body shivers. I feed on connection. On fire. On the current that pours off another body when the restraint burns off, and everything clicks. He gives it freely. Allows me to take as much as I'll ask for, lets me lead even though he's the one setting our pace.

His mouth leaves mine, deserting a thread of wet down my chin, then lower, slower, torturous. He finds the place where my pulse gives me away and lingers there, his tongue resting on it. I swear I feel him number it.

I'm ashamed of how much I need this. How long have I been half-alive, scraping connection from strangers' hands in dark rooms? But when his breath skates over my breasts, the truth buckles in my chest so hard I forget the word for it.

"Elias—" A throaty sound falls out of me before I can catch it. I try to say something coherent. Something that sounds like caution, but it dissolves the second his fingers slip between my thighs.

I'm so fucking wet. Embarrassingly. Shamefully. Or maybe not shamefully at all. Maybe it's the only true thing about me. He already had me once tonight, and for some reason, my body is pleading for more, greedy and unashamed, reaching for him like it hasn't been touched at all.

Elias rises from the couch, yanks his shirt over his head, and tosses it off. His body tightens, a black, unwavering gaze pins me in place, and I finally understand—the darkness in him is appetite. Like mine.

And he's done being gentle.

My body floods with the same wild *yes*.

Elias dives back to me, mouth closing around my breast, and I almost come from the contact alone. My fingers tangle in his hair. The pull of his lips sends thunder roaring through me.

His teeth graze my nipple, drawing a moan out of my throat. He doesn't rush. He savors. Learns me again, piece by piece. One hand holds my hip with stable force, keeping me anchored as he shifts lower, and lower, and—

He's kneeling now, looking at me, spread out before him.

"I don't—" I whisper it. I don't know what I'm trying to say. I don't know how to be wanted like this. I don't know what to do with a look that's decided it's never letting go.

Elias doesn't wait for me to find the words. He lifts my leg over his shoulder with a sure, possessive gentleness. Hands skim down the backs of my thighs, holding me like he's positioning something delicate—something he won't allow himself to damage.

"You're beautiful." His voice slithers down my spine. "You don't know what you do to me."

My whole body curves toward him. The men with open wallets don't come close to this. This man is hungry—but only for what's mine—and that makes me feel *alive* in a way I didn't know I could be.

His mouth finds the inside of my thigh first. Soft kisses. Slow heat. My head tips back. The ceiling comes into view, and stupidly, I register the thin water stain I told my landlord about months ago.

It's near the molding, brown at its edges, the shape of something kneeling—and I shut my eyes because I can't afford whatever that is right now.

Elias moves closer, breath drifting over me. Maddening. *Perfect.*

Parting me with his thumbs, he finds me wet and begging, and when his tongue slips between my slit, I'm done for. Warm lips close around my clit and suck like I'm the sweetest thing he's ever been allowed. He nibbles, then gives a slow, intentional stroke that turns into sparks, and the sparks turn into a fuse.

My fingers tighten in his hair. My hips jerk. His approving groan vibrates into my skin. He's breathing me in, mouth-first, like a man committing a scent to memory. Together, our breathing fractures.

"You taste so fucking good, Rowan. I could eat this pussy forever." His mouth is consuming, exact, slow with a patience I don't understand.

"Jesus—" I whisper, unsure if it's a prayer or praise.

He answers by yanking me closer, grip hardening.

And God, the way he uses his mouth. Demand. Everything I tried to replace in strangers, and never once found.

Body straining toward him, I chase the edge he's building with unbearable precision.

Elias murmurs praise into me, and the obscenity of them hits harder than his tongue. "This pretty little cunt was made for my mouth."

I respond by grinding against him.

"That's it, baby. Ride my face exactly how you've been thinking about it."

The next words are ones I can't quite catch. One sounds like *precious*. One sounds like *mine*. One sounds like a name that isn't mine, but I'm too gone to pull it back out of the air and check.

Tears prick at my eyes. Desire and relief tangled into one overwhelming swell.

"Elias—" My hands hold his head right where I need him. "Right there. Fuck don't stop."

He doubles down. Mouth unyielding. One hand slides up, and two fingers plunge into me. My abs constrict hard enough to hurt. I throw my head back as his mouth works my clit like he's racing against a clock only he can see.

His gaze shoots up. "Come on my tongue, Rowan."

A third finger. "Oh, my God."

His thumb pushes against my bundle of nerves with brute, brief force, then rolls my clit in a tight circle.

I'm writhing, biting my lip, about to come undone. "Fuck —" I pant, laughing, also breaking. I can't take any more. "Stop eating me and fuck me."

Elias stills for a heartbeat. "Not until you make a mess on my mouth, beautiful."

He flattens his tongue and licks up my center once, then

swirls. I'm crashing into him, then his teeth nip my clit, and I go over the edge of a cliff.

"That's it." His fingers pump.

My leg curls around the back of his neck. I'm suffocating him, and he's moaning into me like it's exactly the way he wants to go.

"Make me as wet as you, Rowan. Drown me in your sweet fucking cum."

My nails bite into his skin. Elias groans. The sound of me is unraveling something he'll never recover from. And as the world splinters, one brutal, beautiful truth surfaces underneath:

No one has ever looked at me like this.

I matter to him.

Why?

I don't get to answer it. When the tremors slow, Elias presses one last kiss to the inside of my thigh and stares up at me with a dark glimmer that isn't possession. It isn't lust either. It's more silent. Something that's been patient for a long time.

I've seen this look before, in customers' eyes when they've picked a favorite. When we stop being women to them and start being their obsession.

I tell myself the difference is that Elias has feelings for me. I don't know when I decided to start telling myself that.

Elias rises from the floor, hands sliding up my skin, claiming territory he's already set fire to. "You want to get fucked, Rowan?"

I'm still catching my breath when he kneels back on his heels. Towering over me, chest rising, falling in controlled pulls, the breath of a man who's done this before, who knows how to pace himself, and knows exactly what he has in front of him, his gaze rakes over me and steals whatever strength I have left.

Then he leans down—

and flips me.

It isn't rough. It's firm. *Decisive.* A motion that warns my whole nervous system what's coming.

Palms sinking into the cushions, chest pressing down, the air leaves my lungs in one stunned, broken exhale. My body reacts before I can think, arching, offering.

His hand crawls down my spine, fingertips tracing the curve, the dip, the rise of me. Gentle. *Unbearably* gentle. He's mapping the places he plans to return to.

"So fucking pretty." His thumb sweeps the curve of my hip. Lingers. Twice. Every inch of me feels exposed, like I'm standing in a beam of light and he's the only one allowed to look.

I crane my neck back to look at him. He's watching me with his jaw tense, eyes black, chest heaving. It sends a shiver straight through me, so cold my skin has to chase it down and convert it into want before it becomes anything else.

Elias undoes the button on his jeans, then shoves them and his boxer briefs down and steps out of them. He retrieves a condom, rips it open with his teeth, and rolls it down his thick length.

A second later, heat is at my back. His hands brace either side of my hips. "Is your needy little pussy ready?"

I nod. I've lost my words.

Elias centers me, secures us both. When he pulls me back to position me exactly where he wants, my knees sink deeper into the cushions, and my pulse drums wild beneath my skin. All I can feel is his body aligning behind mine—solid, sure, devastatingly beautiful.

I don't have to see his face to know what's written on it. I feel it in my marrow. And when he blankets himself over me, his mouth brushing the shell of my ear in a slow, torturous drag, his whisper blows me open all over again, "*Mine.*"

Elias pushes into me in one fierce, claiming thrust, and for a split second, everything in me goes white-hot. He doesn't ease me into it. Doesn't grant me a blink, a beat, or a breath to adjust. He breaks through.

A sound tears out of me that isn't coherent language. My body is being split around him, reshaping because it has no other option. "Fuck, Elias."

He straightens, grips my hips, and braces himself against the force of what he's doing. He isn't softening. Or waiting for me to adjust to the shock of his size.

Raw, savage need courses through me. My body takes all of him, though it feels like I'm being torn apart to fit him. I don't care. The truth is—

I want it.

I want him.

Exactly like this.

Elias drives deeper. A cry of pain and pleasure flies out of me. It hurts so fucking good.

"Is this what you wanted, baby?"

"Yes." I'm so lost in what he's doing—how he moves, how he holds me—that I almost miss what's happening inside me. My body surges. Energy ripples through me, bright and urgent, and when I glance down beneath us, I catch the slap of his balls against my clit, and the sight alone almost finishes me.

"You take my cock so fucking good." Elias keeps pumping, reaching further, and every time he pulls me back, he shakes something loose inside me.

My consciousness is tipping, expanding, lifting, as though my soul knows the route to the stars and is dragging the rest of me along for the ride.

His cock barrels through an invisible wall I didn't know existed. The shock of it snatches another cry out of my throat, higher, thinner, the sound a small bird would make if something closed a hand around it.

This is so much dirtier and more ferocious than our first night. And earlier at the club.

"Harder." My spine bows, body yielding like I was made to be wrecked this way.

But this feels evil. Not playful, or reckless, not even just filthy. Sinful. That darkness is looking me full in the face and waiting to see if I'll run. I don't. I stare right back and spread my legs wider. Apparently, there is something deeply wrong with me because all I want is to fuck it and feel it deeper inside.

His hand drags up my stomach, over my ribs, between my breasts. He pinches my nipple and yanks a whimper out of me before his fingers wrap around my throat.

Elias's palm spans the whole of my neck, thumb at my jaw, fingertips brushing the curve behind my ear. He doesn't squeeze, not yet. He holds. Feels. And I realize, dimly, far underneath the pleasure—*he's taking my pulse.*

Attentive, I tell myself again. Present. Here with me.

He's massive. Everywhere. All of him. He slows for one stretched, agonizing moment, with his body pressed to mine, and his mouth on the back of my shoulder.

"Elias, take it—take me."

His fingers tighten around my throat. He rolls his hips, and I lose all cognitive function.

I throw my head back. "Fuck me harder, make me scream. I want it to hurt."

He forces me back down, one hand fisting in my hair, dragging me into the unyielding rhythm he prefers. There's nothing soft in how he's fucking me now. No more patience. All restraint is gone. Only hunger is left, and it's devouring every-thing in its path.

This version of Elias is worlds away from the man who touched me before. That man moved with care, was almost loving, as though I were something breakable.

I don't know which version I crave more.

The Quiet Hand. Or this—the Dark Tide.

One makes me feel chosen.

The other makes me feel claimed.

And somewhere in the space between the two of them, the truth terrifies me most...

I don't want to choose at all.

"Elias," my cry shatters against the cushions.

Each thrust that follows knocks broken, strangled moans out of me. The sharp, rhythmic smack of his body against mine fills the room like applause. His grunts mix with my unravel-ing, and we become a chaotic duet that drowns everything else in the apartment into silence, the fridge, the street, and the thing in me that's been trying to be obedient for years.

Elias isn't worried about that. He's too busy making sure I feel each and every inch of him, over and over, until there's nothing of me that hasn't been touched.

One hand twists in my hair, and he wrenches me back into him, body caging mine while his other hand collars my neck once again.

And I want it. I want all of it. Elias shoves the last rational thought out of my skull, and I let him.

"Every breath you take is mine now." His thrusts turn brutal. Punishing. Power meant to silence the sounds trying to escape me. The couch jolts beneath us. My whimpers splinter into shards. The sound coming out of me isn't human. I can't hold a thought, only pressure and the snap of his control sinking deeper into my spine.

The tension inside me coils viciously, tight enough to hurt, twisting with each brutal force of his hips. I'm right at the edge, skidding toward an orgasm that feels more like destruction than pleasure.

"That's my good fucking girl," he grits it out behind me, voice shredded and dark. He's barely holding himself together.

That's what shoves me over.

"Oh fuck, Elias." My walls clamp down around him. I'm shaking, pleasure ripping through me with an intensity that borders on fear. A cry tears out of my throat. My nails claw the leather. My vision blurs white at the edges.

"Cry into the cushions. No one's going to hear you but me."

I do. Fuck, I do.

Elias loses it a second later, harsh groans bursting out of him as he slams into me one final time, both hands roped in my hair, body locked against mine as he comes apart behind me. Shudders roll through his frame and into mine while hot cum fills the condom inside me.

The world collapses into ragged breathing, shaking limbs, and a fertile silence after, like we shouldn't have done that, but could never have stopped if we'd tried.

His hand stays in my hair for one long heartbeat. Elias exhales, ragged and ruined, and his voice scrapes my ear raw, "I'm nowhere near done with you."

A hand slips beneath my legs. Elias lifts me off the couch and lowers me onto the rug, setting me down with a gentleness that steals my breath. A quivering laugh slips out of me, one full of wonder and exhaustion.

Elias doesn't laugh back. He prowls. That's the only word for it.

Lowering himself down beside me, he pulls the throw from the couch, drapes it over us both, and tucks me against the long line of his chest.

"I'll let you rest for exactly five minutes," he says into my hair. "Then I'm going to make you scream again. Because we still have half an hour before they get here."

I laugh—a small, wrecked thing—and curl into him without meaning to. My body finds a shape against his, as if it were cut to fit.

Behind me, his heart doesn't race. Doesn't slow either. It keeps a patient count against my spine.

Exhaustion drags at me. I fight it.

His thumb finds the pulse at the inside of my wrist. Stays there. Reads.

Attentive, I tell myself for the last time.

My gaze drifts up to the ceiling one last time. In the half-dark, the stain looks less like weeping and more like something watching. I can't shake the sense that I've seen it before. That my sleeping brain is going to spend the night trying to remember where.

I close my eyes.

The last thing I hear, so low I could have dreamed it, is his voice against my temple. *"Four minutes."*

Chapter Ten

ELIAS

THE STAIN on my ceiling has changed shape again. I can't explain why it feels like a face I should recognize.

I've been staring at it from the couch for twenty minutes, one arm over my eyes, the sodden drag of a man who hasn't truly slept in days sitting in my chest. It's spread since the last time I looked—another inch, maybe two—blooming outward, patiently, finding the places in the plaster that were never meant to hold anything and making itself at home there anyway.

Weather does it. Stress does it. Memory does it worst of all.

My phone rings.

The precinct.

I sit up too fast. The room tilts, then steadies. "Ward."

My sergeant exhales. "We've got another one."

The cold comes quickly. It always does. A thread of it sliding down my spine before my brain has finished processing the words. "Location?"

"Sixth Street. Glass façade. Fourth floor."

A flicker moves through me, like a displacement of air in a room with no open windows. "Victim?"

Paper rustles. A pause that lasts one beat too long. "Rowan Townsend."

The world does not tilt this time.

It stops.

My pulse hits the base of my throat hard, like a fist against a door, and then there's nothing. No fridge hum. No traffic from the street below. Nothing at all except silence.

My sergeant's voice drops. "Matches the signature. There's another photograph. Different girl."

The air leaves my lungs.

I gaze up at the ceiling. The stain has stopped spreading. It sits above me, watchful, the five fingers of it splayed wide against the plaster in that familiar reaching posture. It appears, in this moment, to be completely satisfied.

You did well, she says, from the dark wet space. She has sounded like this for years. It's not a voice. More like a soaked cinderblock behind my left eye that's lived there so long I've stopped noticing it.

"Ward." My sergeant barks. "You still with me?"

"Describe the scene."

"Victim on the floor. Asphyxiation. Recent intercourse. No indications of assault." A pause. "Which means whoever did this was possibly someone she knew."

One beat.

Two.

The ceiling watches me with its dark thumb eye.

"How long?"

"ME puts time of death within the last twenty-four hours. Door was left open. Neighbor found her." Another pause. "No one saw anyone enter or leave."

I press my palm flat against my sternum. The pressure there is enormous, a thing with weight and heat that's been building since before the phone rang.

Count. Four in. Four hold. Four out. The only procedure left.

I breathe through it thoroughly, from behind the glass wall I've spent a decade constructing between what I feel and what I show.

"I'll head over."

"Your new partner will meet you there."

That makes me cringe.

"Ward?" His tone makes the hairs on my arms stand on end.

"Yeah?"

"You okay? You sound off."

The anger that moves through me is not the anger I expect. It's not the clean bright anger of a detective who has lost a witness, a person of interest, or a case. It's something older and more protective in a way that has nothing to do with a badge, possessive in a way I do not examine.

"I'm fine," I say. The words feel like gravel in my throat. "I'll be there."

I hang up.

I don't move.

Her scent is still on me. Clove and leather, the sweetness of her lotion, the salt of her skin. It's in the fabric of my hoodie, the shirt I haven't changed, and in the palms of my hands.

Rowan.

I say her name inside my head. It makes no sound at all. The word loses its meaning if you repeat it too many times, like how a face goes strange if you stare at it long enough in a mirror.

Rowan.

Dead.

Except—

I feel her.

She's present, immediate, a warmth in my hands that the morning has not taken, a heaviness in my chest that sits differently than grief. I know grief. I've carried grief for a decade across a hundred crime scenes. I know exactly where it lives, how it moves, and what it costs.

This is not that. I know what grief feels like. This is the wall giving way.

My head throbs. I close my eyes. And the flashes arrive slowly, finding the hidden hollows and filling every space left unguarded.

Her laugh against my throat, breathless, real, nothing like the stage. My hands in her hair. Her nails scoring lines down my back. The floor, the throw blanket pulled down with us, her body curved against mine in the moonlit dark, while the rain hammered the windows.

I open my eyes. The room is still there.

I close them again.

Her fingers. They moved slowly at first. And then the sound—no, not a sound, an absence of sound, the place where sound had been—and my pulse, underneath it all, constant as a metronome, descending to match what was in front of me.

The curve of her cheek, the light of the streetlamp through the curtains, the strips of it falling across the floor, her face, my hand resting on her throat.

The exact moment she stopped being alive.

And started being *kept*.

Not confusion. Recognition.

My eyes open.

I'm standing. I don't remember standing. The room is sharp-edged and bright, the surfaces too detailed, like how a crime scene looks in the first moment before the professional distance engages and the glass wall comes up.

The glass wall is not coming up.

On Rowan's bed, half-hidden in the twisted sheets, a photograph waits where I left it. A new face. Soft mouth. Closed eyes.

But my mind is still on Rowan. The light is most likely drifting across her pretty features now. I watched it fall a hundred times through those curtains, and knew what it would do to the line of her cheek, the base of her throat, and the particular framework of a sleeping woman who does not know she's dreaming for the last time.

I retrieve Rowan's photo from my hoodie and fold it with the care of a man folding something irreplaceable. Crease to crease. Corner to corner. The same way you archive a finished piece. Subjects deserve that much.

It will never leave my possession.

The first one taught me not to leave precious things exposed. The lockbox under the floorboards. The combination I've entered so many times, my fingers move without instruction. The dark interior where the light never reaches.

I slide Rowan inside.

I close the lid.

I stand in the middle of my apartment, breathing, waiting for the professional mask to engage. It doesn't, and I understand dimly that it's not going to, that the glass wall has a crack in it now that was not there before, and something got through.

Above me, the stain spreads another inch.

She was perfect, it says. A pressure sprouts outward, patient and satisfied, as it always is afterward. *I told you she would be.*

I tip my chin up and look at it until my eyes begin to ache.

"Yes," I say, to the ceiling, to the dark wet space behind it, to the thing that lives there that has no name and does not need one. The first time, I said nothing at all. I know better now. "She was."

The streetlamp pushes through the blinds, striping the floor, catching the edge of the stain where it continues its patient, unhurried work against the plaster. I should have patched the damage last month.

My phone is still in my hand.

There is a crime scene waiting for me on Sixth Street.

I am the detective assigned to it.

I take a shower. I dress. I button my coat. I pocket my badge. Uniform before witness. Always.

I close the apartment door behind me with a careful click. I've learned that the most important things are the ones done without witnesses.

The elevator smells of takeout and fabric softener.

I ride it down.

THE POLICE TAPE went up at 9:47 this evening.

I know because I was here when it happened, standing at the corner, surrounded by a city whose sky hasn't decided yet whether it intends to rain, watching the building wake up to the horror it was holding.

The patrol car arrived first. They always do, lights cutting through the dark, two officers moving with the brisk, purposeful energy of people who don't yet know what they're walking into.

Then the second car.

Then the van from the crime lab, which took longer because the people inside already knew what they were walking into and had learned to pace themselves accordingly.

I have always respected that about them.

A crowd gathered, drawn by lights, urgency, and the deep nosy instinct that something has ripped a hole in the fabric of the ordinary. Standing at the perimeter in their coats and their expressions, they held their umbrellas, just in case, and performed concern for each other.

I stood among them, invisible. I am always invisible. I've

learned to look like I belong everywhere and nowhere, noticed by no one.

No one *ever* looks at me.

The bouncer arrived at 10:51.

Devon is his name. I recognized him immediately—the size of him, large, muscular, broad, built like something load-bearing. He came around the corner at speed, phone to his ear, jaw set with tension. He received information his body hadn't yet caught up to.

Devon hit the tape, and the officer stationed there raised a hand. The sound that came out of him was not a word, not quite, something the body produces when the mind has gone white. The wind carried it across the street, and the grief in it brushed a place in me that should have stayed asleep.

Rowan.

Her bouncer fought the officer at the tape for a moment. Then he stopped, sat down on the curb with his elbows on his knees, and his head in his hands.

The officer stood beside him with the helpless posture of someone whose job is to contain things that cannot be contained.

And I watched, noting the mechanics of grief without feeling what a man should feel in its presence. Everything that I actually felt—which was the cold satisfaction of a script, arriving at the end of its movement exactly as written.

She was perfect.

She was exactly as I knew she would be.

I kept my promise.

She lives inside me now, in the dark where the light never reaches, where I keep all my precious things. She is there alongside the wren with the green eyes, and all the others who came before and between, each kept and treasured, more loved in the keeping than they ever were in the living.

Is that not mercy?

The new detective arrived at 11:34.

I noticed her automatically, completely, before the conscious mind finished forming the intention to look. She came from the north, on foot, moving with the compact, purposeful energy of someone who has been called out of sleep and has not wasted time being annoyed about it. Dark coat. Hair pulled back with the practicality of a woman who's decided that mornings are not for aesthetics.

She ducked under the tape and badged the officer at the door without breaking stride. For a moment, in the space between the tape and the entrance, she paused.

She looked at the crowd with a methodical gaze. She understands that the person responsible often cannot resist returning to watch the consequences.

She's right about that.

Her eyes moved across the crowd in a slow, intentional arc. I felt them graze me like a cold draft from a window.

I did not move.

I did not look away.

I simply stood in the shadows, among the grieving civilians with my hands in my pockets, my collar turned up against the dark evening, and looked back at her with the expression of someone watching something terrible happen to someone else's world.

She moved on.

They always move on.

She will be the one who comes the closest, I think. There's something in the quality of that gaze—the patience of it, the precision—that tells me she is not the kind of detective who shoves things away and moves on.

She carries them. Wakes in the night with insomnia,

dealing with a mind that's still working on a problem while the rest of her has agreed to sleep through.

She will be interesting.

I log her away with Devon on the curb, the crime lab van, the tape in the wind. A pattern. A future necessity. All of it is evidence of a story executed with exactness, all of it proof that the work is what I always knew it to be, inevitable, complete.

I turn from the building.

I put my hands deeper in my pockets. I feel the photograph there. It's a replica. I know every detail of it. I chose it to be this way, exactly how I choose evidence, completely, intelligently, and in the dark.

Auburn hair spread across a pink pillow. One hand resting near her throat, fingers slightly curled. A thin gold watch on her wrist that she never removes even in sleep, the face of it catching the light from the window I stood at for fourteen minutes on a Tuesday while she breathed her deep, unaware breaths, and the city moved below us, indifferent as it always is.

She sleeps deeply.

She will not hear me coming.

They never do.

The stain has nothing to say this evening. It does not need to. We are past instruction. The fence holds because I hold it. I am the ground it stands on. I have become what the evil always knew I would. I guess *she* was right.

She always is.

Good, the voice says anyway, from somewhere behind the plaster of the world, in the dark wet space between what is visible and what waits above it. The penny taste of it dissolves familiar on my tongue even here, in the open air, in the night, with the police tape snapping in the wind. *Now bring me someone new.*

I walk north.

Four blocks. Three. Two.

Her building comes into view. A specific arrangement of glass, stone, and light that has become inseparable from the person it houses. Looking at the building is the same as looking at her, the same as standing over her bed, watching her chest rise and fall in that deep unconscious rhythm that belongs entirely to the unaware.

Her living room light is on.

Third floor. Second window from the right. The curtains are white. She leaves them slightly parted because she likes the morning coming through them, which I know because I have watched the morning come through them, which she does not know.

She is home.

She is always home on Thursday nights.

I know everything about her. She takes her coffee black from the place on the corner she visits at exactly eight-fifteen every morning.

I know the smutty book on her nightstand that she's been reading for six weeks because she falls asleep after three pages every night. The bookmark moves forward in increments so small they speak to a woman whose days leave little room for the life she's trying to live.

I know the tattoo on the underside of her left wrist, along with the way she hums to herself in the kitchen when she thinks no one can hear, and the deep sigh she releases when she finally closes the door of her apartment behind her at the end of a long day, releasing all the burdens she carries all day.

She does not know that she has been seen.

She does not know that being seen is about to become the most significant thing that has ever happened to her.

She will understand it eventually.

In the last minutes, in the last breaths, in the exact moment the blue deepens, and the trembling begins, she will appreciate that someone watched. That all that living she did in the ordinary dark was witnessed by *someone* who understood its value when she could not.

Yes. Mercy.

I cross the street.

Like the last, the building requires a code. I have known it for eleven days, learned the way I learn all things—through patient observation, and the simple fact that people are creatures of habit who mistake familiarity for safety.

The elevator smells of someone's greasy takeout, and an industrial cleanliness that suggests a custodian takes their work seriously, which tells me something about the management, which tells me something about the residents, which tells me something about her that I file away alongside everything else I know.

I ride it to three.

The hallway is empty.

Her door is the second on the left.

I stand before it for a moment, just breathing, feeling the wet vibration nest into the base of my skull where it lives, the penny taste dissolving on my tongue, the pressure behind my left eye that has been there so long it's become the baseline against which I measure all other sensation.

The lock takes nine seconds.

I've timed it too.

The apartment smells ordinary. Domestic. The sacred unremarkable machinery of life.

I move through it without turning on a light.

I know it well enough.

In the bedroom, the moonlight comes through. She's so beautiful, asleep in her bed.

This is what the stain taught me to wait for. What the dark asked for in return for all those years of instruction, all those nights of holding the leash, all those mornings of walking away from windows, sitting in the chair beneath the ceiling, and whispering *not tonight* into the empty apartment while it breathed its damp, pleased breath against my temple.

This.

A woman in the evening light, unaware, unguarded, breathing the deep, even breaths.

She has no idea what she is about to become. The eighth study in a series she will never see completed. None of them ever do.

Precious, the stain says. *Kept.*

Yes.

I take her photograph.

I press the shutter.

The click is small in the room's quiet.

She does not stir.

I shove the camera back into my pocket. I look at her for one last moment—black hair, with streaks of blue. A silver nose ring, a slight part to her lips, on a breath she does not know is being counted.

The wet patient thing in my chest opens its eyes, digs into the deep, satisfied sereneness only a monster can have when it has arrived exactly where it always intended to reach. *One more.*

In my apartment, on the wall I keep locked, the composite grows. Images arranged in the shape of a bird in flight. The wings are nowhere near finished. I still have much work to do. She will be the primary feather on the left.

I leave the way I came.

The hallway is still empty. The elevator still smells of

greasy takeout and industrial cleaner. The building door closes behind me with the sound of a held breath finally released.

On the street, I once again turn my collar up against the gray moon. I walk four blocks. The police tape comes into view at the corner of Sixth, still snapping in the wind. The crowd is still there, thinner now, the civilians peeling away as the evening makes its demands, as ordinary life reasserts itself, as it always does in the presence of extraordinary things.

Devon is still on the curb.

He has not moved. He sits with his elbows on his knees, his head still in his hands, and the hush of a large man who has run out of places to put something.

I look at him like how I look at evidence, with appreciation and the cold clarity of a man who understands that devastation is proof of value, that one cannot grieve what was not precious. His grief is, in its own way, a tribute.

Rowan was worth grieving.

I knew that before he did.

The officer at the tape is young. The newer ones are assigned the perimeter while the experienced ones work the interior, which is the correct hierarchy. He straightens when he sees me coming, the instinct of someone who's learned to read a certain kind of approach—the directness of it, the lack of hesitation, the moves a man makes when he has every right to be exactly where he's going.

I'm that man.

I reach into my coat. The badge catches the gray morning light as I flip it open.

The officer lifts the tape without a word.

I duck under it.

Afterword

The Last Frame was always meant to be the beginning of something deeper. The unanswered questions in this story are intentional. The stain on the ceiling. The voice behind the plaster. The badge that should not have cleared that tape. The auburn-haired woman.

These are not loose ends. They are the foundation of what comes next.

Afterimage—the full-length novel continuing the world of *The Last Frame*—is coming. If you need to know whose voice lives behind the stain and how she got there. Or if you need to know how close the new detective gets before it's too late.

You will get your answers.

All of them.

In the meantime, you can find me at: **authorcedarjames.com** and **@authorcedarjames** across all social media platforms.

If *The Last Frame* found its way under your skin, I would be grateful if you left a review. Reviews are how books like this find the readers who need them.

Thank you for entering this darker adventure with me.

—Cedar James

CEDAR JAMES

Contemporary Romance Author

FOLLOW ME ON
social media

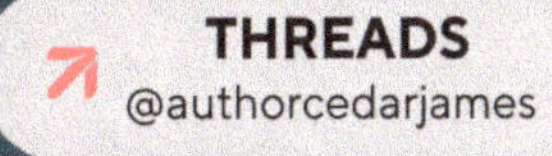

INSTAGRAM
@authorcedarjames

THREADS
@authorcedarjames

TIKTOK
@authorcedarjames

FACEBOOK
@authorcedarjames

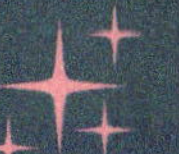

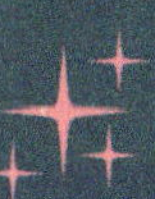

THANKS FOR SUPPORTING
INDIE AUTHORS

Acknowledgments

To my husband, Ben: Thank you for loving me through every version of this dream. As well as the grace, patience, and steady way you hold our life together when I disappear into fictional worlds and come back glassy-eyed, emotionally wrecked, and obsessed with people who do not technically exist. You have been my comfort and my constant. I would not be here without your belief in me, and I will never stop being grateful that I get to walk through this life with you.

To my children: Thank you for sharing your mom with the pages. Without your hugs, laughter, chaos, or your constant reminders of what matters most, I would probably get lost inside these worlds forever. You are my light back home, and the brightest part of my world. Every book I write carries a piece of the love I have for you.

To my family and friends: Thank you for cheering me on, checking in, encouraging me, and reminding me to keep going when the road felt long and impossible. Writing a book may happen at a desk or on the couch, but finishing one takes a village.

To Sarah: Thank you for loving me and all my works. Your support and kind words keep me going when all I feel like doing is stopping. This book—and the other that will come after it—exists because of you.

To my readers: Thank you for taking a chance on this story. And for showing up for my words, characters, and for the dark little corners I dared to explore here. Your messages, reviews, and recommendations, along with every moment you spend with one of my books, mean more than I could ever fully put into words. You are the reason these stories get to breathe beyond my laptop.

To my street team, the Kiss & Tell Club: My loves. You, my critique partners, helped shape this book behind the scenes. Thank you for your honesty, your insight, and your faith in the story, even when it was still rough around the edges. Your fingerprints are on these pages, and I'll cherish that forever.

And finally, to this book, and the strange, shadowed path it carved through me, thank you for asking me to be brave enough to write it.

About the Author

Hey! I'm Cedar James.

Romance writer. Chaos curator. Big-feelings enthusiast.

If you're new here, welcome. If you've been around a while, thank you for sticking with me through banter, heartbreak, swoon, spice, and the occasional genre hop that felt right in my bones.

I write stories that live at the intersection of witty dialogue, emotional intimacy, slow-burn tension, and characters who don't fall in love quietly. My books range from rom-coms that feel like your favorite group chat to darker stories where love has bite.

www.ingramcontent.com/pod-product-compliance
Lightning Source LLC
Chambersburg PA
CBHW052018150726
47999CB00004B/1714